The Violent Enemy

(Previous title:
A Candle for the Dead)

Jack Higgins

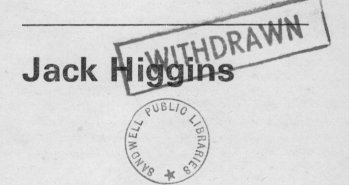

CORONET BOOKS
Hodder and Stoughton

Printed and bound in Great Britain for
Hodder and Stoughton Paperbacks, a
division of Hodder and Stoughton Ltd,
Mill Road, Dunton Green, Sevenoaks,
Kent (Editorial Office: 47 Bedford
Square, London, WC1 3DP) by
Richard Clay (The Chaucer Press) Ltd,
Bungay, Suffolk

ISBN 0 340 10699 9

And this one
for young Sean Patterson

CHAPTER ONE

ON the crest of a tor where the moor lifted to meet the blue sky in a sharply defined edge, Vanbrugh paused to catch his breath, sat on a stone and took out an old briar pipe and a tobacco pouch.

He was a tall, heavily built man in his middle forties, hair greying a little at the temples, shoulders solid with muscle under the old tweed jacket, and carried about him that indefinable quality that only twenty-five years as a policeman gives, a mixture of strength and authority and a shrewdness that was apparent in the light blue eyes.

A few moments later, Sergeant Dwyer joined him and slumped to the ground, chest heaving.

'You should do this more often,' Vanbrugh observed.

'Give me some leave and I will,' Dwyer said. 'I'd like to point out that I've been working a seventy-hour week since February and my last day off was so long ago it's become a fond memory.'

Vanbrugh grinned and put a match to his pipe. 'You shouldn't have joined.'

Somewhere in the distance an explosion echoed flatly on the calm air, and Dwyer sat up quickly. 'What was that?'

'They'll be blasting up at the quarry.'

'Prison working party?'

'That's right.'

Dwyer looked out across the moor, narrowing his eyes into the distance, relaxed and at ease with himself for the first time in months, the sharp, clear air driving the taste of London from his mouth. It was a happy chance that the old man should have chosen to make this mysterious personal visit to the most notorious of Her Majesty's prisons on such a glorious day, but one couldn't help feeling curious.

On the other hand, one thing he had learned in his two years with the Special Branch was that Chief Superintendent Dick Vanbrugh was very much a law unto himself, as many on both sides in the great game had discovered to their cost over the years.

'We'd better be moving,' Vanbrugh said.

Dwyer scrambled to his feet and caught sight of the skeleton of a sheep impaled on a gorse bush in a hollow to the left.

'Death in life, even here on a day like this.'

'No escaping it wherever you go.' Vanbrugh turned and looked across the moor again. 'Whenever the mist creeps in, this place becomes a waking nightmare. A man can walk all day and end where he began.'

'No one ever gets off the moor,' Dwyer said softly. 'Isn't that what they say?'

'Something like that. In the whole history of the place, there's only one recorded instance of a man getting clean away and he's probably lying at the bottom of a bog. Some of them could swallow a three-ton truck.'

'The right sort of place for a prison.'

'That's what they thought when they built it.'

Vanbrugh set off down the slope towards the car parked at the side of the narrow road below and Dwyer followed, stumbling over the tussocks of rough grass and patches of marshy ground, water seeping in through the laceholes of his smart town brogues.

When he reached the car, Vanbrugh was already sitting in the passenger seat and Dwyer climbed behind the wheel, pressed the starter and drove away.

He was hot and tired, his feet were wet and his sweat-soaked shirt clung to his back. A small spark of temper flared inside him, but he pushed it away with a determined effort.

8

'A one-hundred-and-seventy-mile drive, wet feet and the makings of a good sprain in my ankle. I hope he's worth it, sir.'

Vanbrugh turned sharply and the blue eyes were very cold. '*I* think so, Sergeant.'

Dwyer took a deep breath, aware that one of those violent storms for which Dick Vanbrugh was so notorious was about to break over his head, but the moment passed. Vanbrugh applied another match to the bowl of his pipe and Dwyer concentrated on his driving and on the sheep and wild ponies which frequently wandered across the unfenced road. Ten minutes later they came over a slight rise and saw the prison in the hollow below.

The moors lifted in a purple swell fading almost imperceptibly into the horizon, and at the head of the quarry a red flag danced in the slight breeze.

The explosion, when it came, echoed into the distance, the sound of it beating against the hills like thunder. As a great shoulder of rock cracked into a thousand pieces, smoke drifted in a white pall that curled over the edge of the rock and across the moor like some living thing.

A whistle sounded, and as the convicts emerged from shelter a Land-Rover came over the edge of the escarpment, rolled down the dirt road and stopped.

The youth at the wheel had very fair hair and blue eyes that somehow made him look even younger than he was. His uniform was brand new and he was painfully conscious of that fact as he got out of the Land-Rover and moved past a group of convicts loading a truck.

Mulvaney, the Duty Officer, moved to meet him, a black and tan Alsatian at his heels. He grinned. 'Hello, Drake. Putting you to work already, are they?'

Drake nodded. 'I've got a chit here for a man called Rogan. The Governor wants to see him.'

He produced a slip of paper from his breast pocket. Mulvaney initialled it and waved towards a small hollow at the bottom of the slope.

'That's Rogan down there. You're welcome to him.'

The man indicated worked stripped to the waist and was at least six foot three, the muscles in his broad back rippling as he swung a sledgehammer above his head and brought it down.

'God in heaven, the man's a giant,' Drake said.

Mulvaney nodded. 'They don't come much bigger. Brains and brawn, that's Sean Rogan. Pound for pound, about the most dangerous man we've ever had in here.'

'They didn't send anyone with me.'

'No need. He's expecting his discharge any day now. That'll be what the Governor wants to see him about. He's hardly likely to make a run for it at this stage.'

Drake moved down the slope. Bronzed and fit, his body toughened by hard labour, Sean Rogan looked a thoroughly dangerous man and the ugly puckered scars of the old bullet wounds in the left breast seemed strangely in keeping.

Drake paused a yard or two away and Rogan glanced up. The skin was stretched tightly over high Celtic cheekbones, a stubble of beard covering the hollow cheeks and strong pointed chin. The eyes were grey like water over a stone or smoke through trees on an autumn day, calm and expressionless, holding their own secrets. It was the face of a soldier, a scholar perhaps. Certainly this was no criminal.

'Sean Rogan?' Drake said.

The big man nodded. 'That's me. What do you want?'

There was no hint of subservience in the soft Irish voice and Drake, for some unaccountable reason, felt like a young recruit being interviewed by a senior officer.

'The Governor wants a word with you.'

Rogan picked up his shirt from a nearby boulder, pulled it over his head and followed Drake up the slope, the sledgehammer swinging easily in one hand. He dropped it beside the Duty Officer. 'A present for you.'

Mulvaney grinned, took a battered silver case from his breast pocket and offered him a cigarette. 'Is it likely at all, Sean Rogan, that I might be seeing the back of you?'

Rogan's face was illuminated briefly by a smile of great natural charm. 'All things are possible, even in this worst of all possible worlds. You should know that, Patrick.'

Mulvaney touched him briefly on the shoulder. 'Go with God, Sean,' he said softly in Irish.

Rogan turned and walked quickly towards the Land-Rover and Drake found himself trailing a step or two behind. As they passed the group of convicts loading the truck, someone shouted, 'Good luck, Irish!' Rogan raised a hand in reply and climbed into the passenger seat.

Drake got behind the wheel and drove away rapidly, feeling uncertain and ill-at-ease. It was as if Rogan had taken charge, as if at any moment he might order him to take the next turning on the right instead of keeping straight on to the prison.

The Irishman smoked his cigarette slowly from long habit, gazing out over the moor. Drake glanced sideways at him a couple of times and tried to make conversation.

'They tell me you're hoping to get out soon?'

'One can always hope.'

'How long have you been here?'

'Seven years.'

The shock of it was like a blow in the face and Drake winced, thinking of the long years, the wind across the moor blowing rain, grey mornings, a brief summer passing quickly into autumn and the iron hand of winter.

He forced a smile. 'I've only been here a couple of days myself.'

'Your first posting?'

'No, I was at Wakefield for a while. Came out of the Guards last year. Didn't fancy another hitch and then I saw this advert for prison officers. It looked a good number so I thought I'd try it.'

'Is that a fact now?'

For some unaccountable reason Drake felt himself flushing. 'Somebody has to do it,' he said defensively. 'The pay could be worse and quarters and a pension at the end of it. You can't grumble at that, can you?'

'I'd rather be the devil,' Sean Rogan said with deep conviction. He half-turned, folding his arms deliberately, and stared out across the moor, cutting off all further attempts at conversation.

'It's certainly one hell of a record,' the Governor said, looking down at the file on his desk, 'but then I don't need to tell you that, Superintendent. I was hoping we'd see the back of him this time.'

'So was I, sir,' Vanbrugh said.

'There are days when I distinctly welcome the fact that I retire in another ten months.' The Governor pushed back his chair and stood up. 'He'll be here in about fifteen minutes. In the meantime, I've one or two things to do. You make yourselves comfortable in here and I'll have them send you in some tea.'

The door closed behind him and Dwyer moved from the window to the desk. 'I don't know a great deal about Rogan, sir. A bit before my time. Wasn't he a big man in the I.R.A.?'

'That's right. Sentenced to twelve years in '56 for organizing escapes from several prisons in England and Ulster. Remember the famous invasion of Peterhead in '55? They went over the wall under cover of darkness like blasted commandos and brought out three men. Got clean away.'

'He was behind that?'

'He led them in.' Vanbrugh opened the file. 'It's all here. He spent most of his early life in France and Germany. His father was in the Irish political service. He was a student at Trinity College, Dublin, when he was wounded and caught during a weekend raid over the Ulster border. That would be just before the war.'

'What did he get?'

'Seven years. He was released in 1941 at the request of the Special Operations Executive because of his fluency in French and German. That's when I first came across

12

him. I was working for them myself at the time. He was given the usual training and dropped into France to organize the Maquis in the Vosges Mountains. He did damned well, saw the war out, told them what to do with their medals and demobbed himself the moment it was over.'

'What did he do then?'

'Got up to his old tricks. Five years at Belfast in 1947. They let him off lightly because of his war record. Not that it made any difference. He escaped within a year.' Vanbrugh grinned wryly. 'He made a habit of that. Parkhurst in '56, but never got off the island. Peterhead the following year. Three days on foot across the moor, then the dogs ran him down.'

'Which explains why he was finally sent here?'

'That's it. Maximum security. No possibility of escape.' Vanbrugh started to fill his pipe again. 'If you examine the file you'll find a confidential entry at the back. It refers to an incident the Commissioners prefer to keep quiet about. In July 1960 Sean Rogan was picked up in the early hours of the morning crossing the field at the rear of the officers' quarters.'

Dwyer frowned. 'Isn't that outside the wall?'

Vanbrugh nodded. 'The principal officer had been playing cards late at another house. He had his Alsatian with him and on the way home, it picked up Rogan's scent.'

'But how did he get out?'

'He wouldn't say. The Commissioners wanted it kept out of the press so the enquiry was very hush-hush. It was finally decided that he must have hidden himself in a car or truck on its way out.'

'At that time in the morning?'

'Don't worry. No one really accepted that one. They had him on maximum security for a couple of years after that. When the Governor finally made things a little easier for him, Rogan told him that it didn't matter because he wasn't going to try again. He said that getting out was easy. It was getting anywhere without help once you were out that was difficult. I think he decided to sweat out his sentence and hope for remission.'

'Which is what he's just applied for?'

Vanbrugh nodded. 'When the I.R.A. called off its border campaign in Ulster recently it just about went into liquidation. Most of its members serving sentences in English gaols have since been released. In fact the Home Office has been under considerable pressure to release them all.'

'And what's the answer on Rogan?'

'They're still frightened to death of him. Now I've got to tell him he's still got five years to serve.'

'Why you, sir?'

Vanbrugh shrugged. 'We worked together during the war. Since then, I've arrested him on three separate occasions. You might say I'm the Yard's Rogan expert.'

He walked to the window and stood looking out into the courtyard. 'England's the only country in the civilized world that doesn't make special provision for political offenders, did you know that, Sergeant?'

'I hadn't really given it much thought, sir.'

'You should do, Sergeant. You should do.'

The door opened and the Governor came in quickly. 'They're bringing him up now.' He sat down behind his desk and grinned tightly. 'I really don't have much stomach for this one, Superintendent. I'm glad you're here.'

The door opened again and the Principal Officer came in. 'He's here, sir.'

The Governor nodded. 'Let's get it over with, then.'

Outside, Drake stood beside the door waiting, and Rogan leaned against the wall, arms folded as he stared through the window at the end of the corridor.

Life was, on the whole, an act of faith. He'd read that somewhere once, but twenty years of hard living, of violence and the dark places had taught him to look only for the unexpected on the other side of each new hill.

14

Everyone in the place, including the screws, expected his pardon to go through. To Rogan, that was sufficient reason in itself for something to go wrong. When the door opened and the Principal Officer called him in, he was prepared for the worst.

The presence of Vanbrugh confirmed what was already apparent from the atmosphere in the office, and he stood in front of the desk, hands behind his back and looked out of the window over the Governor's head. He noticed that the trees on the hill beyond the wall were stripped quite bare of leaves now and the untidy nests of the rookery were clearly exposed to view. He watched a rook flap lazily through the air from one tree to another and became aware that the Governor was speaking to him.

'We've had a communication from the Home Office, Rogan. Chief Superintendent Vanbrugh brought it down with him specially.'

Rogan turned slightly to face Vanbrugh, and the big policeman got to his feet, suddenly awkward. 'I'm sorry, Sean. Damned sorry.'

'Then there's nothing to be said, is there?'

The hard shell with which he had surrounded himself was something they could not penetrate. In the heavy silence, the Governor glanced helplessly at Vanbrugh, then sighed.

'I think you'd better come in from the quarry for a while, Rogan.'

'Permanently, sir?' Rogan said calmly.

The Governor swallowed hard. 'We'll see how you go on.'

'Very well, sir.'

Rogan turned and walked to the door without waiting for the Principal Officer's order. He stood in the corridor, face expressionless, aware of the murmur of voices as the door closed behind him.

'You can go now, Drake,' the Principal Officer said, then turned to Rogan and said briskly, 'All right, Rogan.'

They went downstairs and crossed the courtyard to one

of the blocks. Rogan stood waiting for the door to be unlocked, aware from the expression on the Duty Officer's face that he knew, which wasn't particularly surprising. Within another half hour every con, every screw in the place would know.

The prison had been constructed in the reform era of the nineteenth century on a system commonly found in Her Majesty's prisons. Half a dozen three-tiered cell blocks radiated like the spokes of a wheel from a central hall which lifted a hundred feet into the gloom to an iron framed dome.

For reasons of safety each cell block was separated from the central hall by a curtain of steel mesh. The Principal Officer unlocked the gate into D block and motioned Rogan through.

They mounted an iron staircase to the top landing, boxed in with more steel mesh to prevent anyone who felt like it from taking a dive over the rail. His cell was at the far end of the landing and he paused, waiting for the Principal Officer to unlock the door.

As it opened, Rogan took a step forward and the Principal Officer said, 'Don't try anything silly. You've everything to lose now.'

Rogan swung round, his iron control snapping for a brief moment so that the man recoiled from the savage anger that blazed in the grey eyes. He slammed the door shut quickly, turning the key in the lock.

Rogan turned slowly. The cell was only six by ten with a small barred window, and a washbasin and fixed toilet had been added in an attempt at modernization. A single bed ran along each wall.

A man was lying on one of them reading a magazine. He looked about sixty-five, with very white hair, and eyes a vivid blue in a wrinkled humorous face.

'Hello, Jigger,' Rogan said.

In that single moment, the smile died on Jigger Martin's face and he swung his legs to the floor. 'The bastards,' he said. 'The lousy rotten bastards.'

16

Rogan stood looking out through the small barred window and Martin produced a packet of cigarettes from beneath his mattress and offered him one. 'What are you going to do now, Irish?'

Rogan blew out a cloud of smoke and laughed harshly. 'What do you think, boyo? What do you think?'

As the gates closed behind them, Dwyer was conscious of a very real relief. It was as if a great weight had been lifted from him, and he took out his cigarettes.

He offered one to Vanbrugh who was driving, his face dark and sombre, but the big man shook his head. When they reached the crest of the hill, he braked, turned and looked down at the prison.

Dwyer said softly, 'What do you think he'll do, sir?'

Vanbrugh swung round, all his pent-up frustration and anger boiling out of him. 'For God's sake, use your intelligence. You saw him, didn't you? There's only one thing a man like that can do.'

He moved into gear and drove away rapidly in a cloud of dust.

CHAPTER TWO

DURING most of September it had been warm and clear, but on the last day the weather broke. Clouds hung threateningly over the moor, rain dripped from the gutters and when Rogan went to the window, brown leaves drifted across the courtyard from the trees in the Governor's garden.

Behind him Martin shuffled the cards on a small stool. 'Another hand, Irish?'

'Not worth it,' Rogan said. 'They'll be feeding us soon.' He stood at the window, a slight frown on his face, his eyes following the roof line of the next block to the hospital beyond, and Martin joined him.

'Can it be done, Irish?'

Rogan nodded. 'It can be done all right. It took me just over two hours last time.' He turned and looked down at Martin. 'You'll never make it, Jigger. You'd break your bloody neck halfway.'

Martin grinned. 'What would I be wanting to crash out for? Nine months and I can spit in their eyes once and for all. My old woman's got a nice little boarding house going in Eastbourne. They won't see me back here again.'

'I seem to have heard that one before,' Rogan said. 'Can you still work that trick of yours on the door?'

'Always happy to oblige.'

Martin took an ordinary spoon from his bedside locker and went to the door. He listened for a moment, then dropped to one knee.

The lock was covered by a steel plate perhaps six inches square, and he quickly forced the handle of the spoon between the edge of the plate and the jamb. He worked it around for several minutes and there was a slight click. He pulled and the door opened slightly.

'Now that's one thing that always impresses me,' Rogan said.

'There's thirty years' hard graft there, Irish. The best screwsman in the business.' Martin sighed. 'The trouble is I got so good they could always tell when it was me.'

He pushed the door gently into place and worked the spoon round again. There was another slight click and he stood up.

'There have been times in my life when I could have used you,' Rogan said.

'You don't want to start consorting with criminals at your age, Irish.' Martin grinned. 'An old lag's trick. Plenty of cons in this place could do as much. These old

18

mortice deadlocks are a snip. One of these days they'll get wise and change them.'

He went back to his bed, produced a packet of cigarettes and tossed one across to Rogan. 'There's at least six other gates to pass through between here and the yard and most of them are guarded, remember. It'll take more than a spoon to get you out of this place.'

'Anything can be done if you put your mind to it,' Rogan said. 'Come to the window and I'll show you.'

Martin held up a hand quickly and shook his head. 'Nothing doing. What I don't know can't hurt you.'

Rogan frowned. 'You're no grass, Jigger.'

The old man shrugged. 'We can all be pushed just so far in a place like this.'

There was a rattle at the door and, turning quickly, Rogan was aware of an eye at the spyhole. The key turned in the lock and the Principal Officer came in.

'Outside, Rogan. Someone wants to see you.'

Rogan frowned. 'Who is it?'

'A bloke called Soames. Lawyer from London. Something to do with an appeal. Seems you've got friends working for you.'

As he waited in the queue outside the visiting room, Rogan wondered about Soames, trying to decide what could be behind his visit. As far as he was aware, there was no chance of an appeal against the Home Secretary's decision for at least another year, and to his certain knowledge there was no one working for him on the outside. Since the Organization had gone into voluntary liquidation the previous year, he'd become a dead letter to most people.

When his turn came, the Duty Officer took him in and sat him in a cubicle. Rogan waited impatiently, the conversation on either side a meaningless blur, and then the door opened and Soames came in.

He was small and dark with a neatly trimmed moustache and soft pink hands. He carried a bowler hat and briefcase and wore a neat pin-striped suit.

He sat down and smiled through the wire mesh. 'You won't know me, Mr. Rogan. My name's Soames—Henry Soames.'

'So I've been told,' Rogan said. 'Who sent you?'

Soames glanced each way to make sure that no individual conversation could be overheard in the general hubbub, then leaned close.

'Colum O'More.'

A vivid picture jumped into Rogan's mind at once, one of those queer tricks that memory plays. He had just volunteered to 'go active' as they'd called it in the Organization in those days, a callow, seventeen-year-old student. They'd taken him to a house outside Dublin for the final important interview and had left him alone in a small room to wait. And then the door had opened and a giant of a man had entered, the mouth split in a wide grin as he laughed back over his shoulder at someone outside, wearing his strength and courage for all to see like a suit of armour. Colum O'More—the Big Man.

'Are you sure, *avic*?' he'd said to Rogan. 'You know what you're getting into?'

Mother of God, who wouldn't be sure and face to face with such a man?

'So Colum sent you?' Rogan said.

'Not directly.' Soames smiled faintly. 'I believe there's something like half of a ten-year sentence still hanging over his head in this country. He *is* in England at the moment, but we've only met personally once. Since then I've been working through an accommodation address.'

'If you're thinking of raising my case again with the Home Secretary, you're wasting your time.'

'I couldn't agree more.' Soames smiled slightly. 'To be perfectly frank, Colum O'More was thinking of adopting more unorthodox means.'

'Such as?' Rogan said calmly.

'Assisting you to leave without the Home Secretary's permission.'

'And what makes you think I could?'

'A man called Pope,' Soames said. 'I believe he shared a cell with you for a year? He was released six months ago.'

'I still have the stink of him in my nostrils,' Rogan said contemptuously. 'A cheap, two-a-penny tearaway. The worst kind. Was a peeler with the Metropolitan and got done for corruption. He'd sell his own sister on the streets if you made it worth his while.'

'He tells an interesting story, Mr. Rogan. He insists that in 1960 you were caught in the early hours of the morning outside the walls of this prison. That to this day the authorities have never been able to find out how you got out.'

'He has a big mouth,' Rogan said. 'One day someone will be closing his eyes with pennies.'

'Is it true?' Soames said, and for the first time there was an urgency in his voice. 'Have you a way out?'

'And if I had?'

'Then Colum O'More would be glad to see you.'

'And how could that be managed?'

Soames leaned even closer. 'You know the quarry and the hamlet between it and the river—Hexton?'

'I've been working there for the past year.'

'Below the quarry there's an iron footbridge. On the other side of the river you'll find a cottage. You can't miss it. It's completely isolated.'

'Will Colum be there?'

'No, Pope.'

'Why him?'

'He's proved very useful. He'll have clothes, a car, even an identity for you. You could be clear of the moor within half an hour.'

'And where do I go?'

'Pope will have full instructions. They'll take you to Colum O'More. That's as much as I can tell you.'

Rogan sat there, a slight frown knitting his forehead, considering the situation. He wasn't happy about Pope, and Soames was a hollow man if ever he'd seen one, but was there really any choice? And if Colum O'More was behind the organization . . .

'Well?' Soames said.

Rogan nodded. 'How soon can Pope be ready?'

'He's ready now. I'd heard you were a man who doesn't like to let grass grow under your feet.'

'It's Thursday today,' Rogan said. 'Better make it Sunday.'

'Any particular reason?'

'It's dark by six and we're locked up for the night at half past in my wing. From then on there's only one duty screw who works from the central hall checking blocks. If I'm not missed, and there's no reason why I should be, they won't find I'm gone till they turn out the cells at seven on Monday morning.'

'Which sounds sensible.' Soames hesitated and then said carefully, 'You're certain you can get out?'

'Nothing's certain in this life, Mr. Soames, I'd have thought you'd have found that out for yourself by now.'

'How right you are, Mr. Rogan.' Soames picked up his bowler hat and briefcase and pushed back his chair. 'I don't think there's anything more to discuss. I'll look forward to Monday's newspaper with interest.'

'So will I,' Rogan said.

He stood there watching as Soames walked to the door and waited. A few moments later, the Principal Officer came for him and they went back into the corridor.

As they went back across the courtyard, he said, 'Any joy?'

Rogan shrugged. 'You know what these lawyers are like. Big with their promises and fees, but short on hope. I gave up counting my chickens a long time ago.'

'The best way of looking at things and the most sensible.'

When they reached the top landing, the bell was sounding for the midday meal and when Rogan went back into his cell, Martin already had the plates ready on the small table. When the door closed, he waited for a moment, then looked at Rogan questioningly.

'And what was all that about?'

For a moment, Rogan was going to tell him and then he remembered the old man's words earlier. That in a place like this a man could only be pushed so far. He was right, of course. If Sean Rogan had learned one thing from the thirteen years of his life spent between four walls, it was that no one was ever completely dependable.

He shrugged. 'Some friends of mine on the outside have clubbed together and dug up a lawyer. He wanted to meet me personally before trying the Home Secretary again.'

Martin's face creased into the perpetual smile of hope of the long serving convict. 'Hell, Irish, maybe things are looking up.'

'You can always hope,' Sean Rogan said and moved to the window.

It was still raining and a slight mist curled across the top of the hill beyond the walls where the quarry lay. If you listened carefully you could almost hear the river; dark, peat-stained, splashing over great boulders on its long run down to the sea.

CHAPTER THREE

RAIN dashed against the window as Rogan peered into the darkness. After a while, he went to the door and stood listening, and from below the steel gate clanged hollowly as the Duty Officer closed it after him.

He turned and grinned tightly, his face shadowed in the dim light. 'A hell of a night for it.'

Martin was lying on his bed reading a book, and he pushed himself up on one elbow. 'For what?'

Rogan crouched beside him and said calmly, 'I'm crashing out, Jigger. Whose side are you on?'

'Why, yours, Irish, you don't need to ask.' The old man's face was grey with excitement and he swung his legs to the floor. 'What do you want me to do?'

'Open the door,' Rogan said. 'Just that. When I've gone, you leave it unlocked, get back on your bed and stay there till they turn out the cells at seven.'

Martin licked his lips nervously. 'What happens when they bring me up in front of the Governor?'

'Tell him you got the shock of your life when I opened the door, that you lay there and minded your own business.' Rogan grinned coldly. 'After all, that's just what he'd expect you to do. Any con who did anything else under similar circumstances wouldn't last twenty-four hours before the boys got to him. The Governor knows that as well as you do.'

The threat was implicit and Martin got to his feet hastily. 'Hell, Irish, I wouldn't do anything to ball things up, you know that.'

Rogan turned over his mattress, slid his hand through the seam at one side and pulled out a coil of nylon rope and a sling with snap links at the end, of the type used by climbers.

'Where in the hell did you get those?' Martin asked.

'They use them up at the quarry when they're placing charges in the cliff face.' Rogan took out a narrow-handled screwdriver and a pair of nine-inch wire cutters which he tucked into his belt.

'These came by way of the machine shop.' He nodded towards the door. 'Okay, Jigger, let's get moving. I'm on a tight schedule.'

Martin took out the spoon and knelt in front of the door, his hands shaking a little. For a moment he seemed to be having some difficulty and then there was a slight click. He turned, his face very pale in the dim light, and nodded.

Rogan quickly arranged his pillow and some spare

clothing from his locker into some semblance of a human form under the blankets on his bed. He moved to the door.

'I just thought of something,' Martin said. 'You know how the duty screw pussyfoots around in carpet slippers?'

'He'll have a look through the spyhole, that's all,' Rogan said, 'and if he can tell that it isn't me in that bed in this light, he's got better eyes than I have.'

Suddenly, Martin seemed to undergo a change. It was as if ten years had slipped from his worn shoulders and he laughed softly. 'I can't wait to see the expression on that screw's face in the morning.' He clapped Rogan on the shoulder. 'Go on, son, get to hell out of it and keep on running.'

The landing was dimly lit and the wing was wrapped in quiet. Rogan stood in the shadow of the wall for a moment, then moved quickly to the stairs at the far end.

The great central hall was illuminated by a single light, and above him its roof and the dome were shrouded in darkness. He climbed on to the rail and scrambled up the steel mesh curtain to the roof of the cell block. He hooked the snap links of his sling into the wire, securing himself in place and took out the wire cutters.

It didn't take him long, cutting in a straight line against the wall, to make an aperture perhaps three feet long through which he pulled himself. Once on the other side, he again hooked himself into place and carefully closed up the links one by one so that only a close inspection could reveal his passage. His previous escape had been made from B block on the opposite side of the hall and in three years no one had discovered his route out from there.

Steel supporting beams lifted into the darkness, each one supported on a block of masonry which jutted from the main fabric of the wall. He reached the first one with ease and wedged himself against the wall, judging the five foot gap to the next carefully. A quick breath, a leap into darkness and he was across. He repeated the performance three times until he had completed the necessary half-circle which brought him to the beam close to B block.

A door clanged and he glanced down and saw the Duty Officer and the Chief walk through the pool of light below to the desk. They were talking together in low tones, the voices drifting up as the Duty Officer made an entry in the night book. There was a burst of laughter and they crossed the hall, unlocked the door leading to the guardroom and disappeared.

Rogan slipped the sling around the beam and his waist, snapped the links together and started to climb, leaning well out.

The difficulty lay in the fact that the beam itself started to curve, following the line of the wall, leaving only an inch or two for the sling. It was now that his perfect physical condition and massive strength stood him in good stead. He gritted his teeth and heaved his way up into the darkness almost inch by inch and the pool of light receded beneath him. A few moments later, he reached his objective, a large steel ventilation grille, perhaps two and a half feet square.

It was held in place by two large screws on either side and he braced himself against the wall, leaning back in the sling, took out the screwdriver and set to work.

The screws were brass and came out easily, but he left one partly in position so that the grille swung down, no longer obscuring the entrance, but still securely held.

He had now reached the most difficult moment. He carefully unhooked the spring links securing the sling and pushed it into the shaft quickly, then forcing his fingers behind the beam he walked up the wall and pushed himself feet first into the zinc-lined ventilating shaft. Clouds of dry dust arose, filling his nostrils. He choked back a cough and reached out and swung the grille back into place. Very carefully he pushed his fingers through and replaced the screw he had removed, covering his tracks completely.

On his previous attempt he'd had an electric torch,

something he hadn't managed to get hold of this time, and from now on he had to work in darkness, relying completely on memory.

He had worked out the route after a fast ten minutes with a map of the prison's ventilation system carelessly left on a bench in the machine shop by a heating engineer, but that had been three years ago and there had been structural alterations since then. He could only pray that the section he was using had been left alone.

He moved backwards into darkness, the dust filling his eyes and throat, sweat trickling down his face, and after a while, came to another opening. He went into it head first and slid gently down a shallow slope, slowing his descent by bracing his hands against the sides.

At the bottom, he paused. It was completely dark, no chink of light anywhere. He was boxed in as securely as if he had been in his own coffin. He pushed the idea away from him and inched forward again.

He came to a side shaft and then another and paused. Six or was it seven? No, six before he roped down to the first level. He pushed forward again, counting until he reached the shaft on his left. He ran his hand along the right side and found at once the supporting bracket he had forced from the wall as a support on that other occasion. He pushed forward, then eased himself backwards into the hole. He supported himself with his arms, uncoiled the nylon rope, looped it into a running line around the bracket he had forced out from the wall, then lowered himself carefully down the shaft. Thirty feet below, it curved into a straight line and he moved into it backwards on his belly, pulling the rope down after him. He coiled it carefully and inched backwards.

Light showed through in several places and he paused at a grille and peered down into the main kitchens. There was a light on, but they were quite deserted and he moved on, emerging into a slightly larger shaft. He twisted round and went forward on his hands and knees.

He was now at the far end of the central block and

perhaps forty minutes had elapsed since he left his cell. He moved on quickly and came out into the bottom of a wide shaft that lifted vertically above his head, bands of yellow light cutting into it from grilles set at several levels.

The zinc lining of the shaft was held in place by a network of steel stays which provided excellent footholds and he started to climb quickly. His objective was a side shaft at the very top which ran through the roof and out across the courtyard to the hospital on the other side.

He became conscious of a strong current of air and a low, humming sound, and frowned. This was something new and the heart moved inside him. A few moments later he reached the top of the shaft and his worst fears were confirmed. Where there had previously been only the entrance to the link with the hospital, there was now a metal grille protecting an electric extractor fan. He stayed there for a moment, tracing the edge of the grille with his free hand, knowing it was hopeless, then started down.

The first grille he came to was only a foot square and he moved on down to the next. This was perhaps two feet square, a tight squeeze certainly, but possible. He could see into a quiet corridor, dimly lit and remembered that these would be the bachelor quarters for unmarried officers.

He hesitated for only a moment, wedged there in the narrow shaft, then took out the screwdriver and pushed his hand as far between the bars of the grille as it would go, holding the screwdriver by the shaft. He felt for the head of the left hand screw and to his relief it started to move at once. A moment later, the screw fell to the floor and he forced the grille down with all his strength.

He went back up the shaft a little way so that he was able to lower himself through the grille feet first. There wasn't much room, and for a moment he seemed to stick and then went through in a rush, shirt tearing, landing six feet below in the corridor.

He picked himself up quickly, turned and forced the grille back into position, then moved along the corridor. He could hear a radio playing and there was a quick burst of laughter, strangely muted and far away. At the end of the corridor, he came to the stairhead and looked over the banisters. Three floors below he could see the entrance hall quiet and still in the light from a single yellow bulb. He went down quickly, keeping to the wall.

At the bottom he paused in the shadows, then crossed quickly to the door, then opened it and hesitated in the porch. A lamp jutted from the wall, casting a pool of light to the path below, and he went down the steps quickly and moved into the darkness at the front of the walls.

The rain was falling heavily now, bouncing from the cobbled courtyard like steel rods and he glanced up at the ventilating shaft high above his head stretching across to the hospital. It had originally given him access to the hospital roof, now he had to find another route.

He kept to the shadows of the wall, working his way round the courtyard until he reached the hospital and moved round to one side. It was then that he remembered the fire escape. He found it a moment later and started quickly, head lowered against the driving rain.

The final landing was outside a door directly under the eaves of the roof and he climbed on to the rail, reached up to the gutter and tested it quickly. It seemed reasonably secure and he took a quick breath and heaved himself up and over.

He scrambled up on to the ridge of the building and moved along it, a foot on either side, hands braced against the tiles. It took him a good five minutes of careful work to reach the end of the building and the chimney stack of the incinerator.

No more than fifty feet away from him through the darkness was the spiked edge of the outer wall of the prison, and beneath him an iron drainage pipe cut through space to meet it. Rogan uncoiled his nylon rope, flung one end round the chimney stack and went straight over the edge gripping the double strand tightly.

His feet slipped on wet brickwork and he swung wildly, skinning his knuckles and bruising his shoulder painfully and then his legs banged against the pipe.

He sat on it, legs astride, and pulled the rope down, coiling it again, then he started across. The narrow pipe cut into his crotch and he moved painfully on, pushing away the thought of the cobbles forty feet below, concentrating on the task in hand. Was it now, or was it three years previously? There was no way of telling and life seemed a circle turning upon itself endlessly. His fingers touched stone and he looked up to see the darker line of the wall against the sky.

He carefully stood up, reached for the rusty spikes and pulled himself on top. With hardly a pause, he uncoiled the rope, looped it around a couple of spikes and went over the edge, using the same double strand technique as in descending from the hospital roof. A few moments later he dropped ten feet into wet grass at the foot of the wall, pulling the rope down after him.

He was soaked to the skin and for a moment he lay there, his face in the coolness of the wet grass and then he scrambled to his feet. He coiled the nylon rope quickly, hooked it over his head, turned and moved quickly away through the darkness.

Remembering his previous experience, he gave the married quarters a wide berth, striking up the hillside to the open moor and the quarry.

Darkness was his friend and five minutes later he reached the crest of the valley and paused to look back. Below in the hollow the prison lay like some primeval monster crouching in the darkness, shapeless, without form, a yellow light gleaming here and there and at its feet the houses crouched.

Rogan was suddenly filled with a fierce exhilaration. He laughed out loud, turned and started to run across the moor. It took him fifteen minutes to reach the quarry and beyond it, the river, swollen by rain, tumbled over boulders in the darkness.

Halfway across the iron footbridge, he paused and tossed the rope, screwdriver and wirecutters into the foam. Somehow there was a finality about the act. This time there would be no going back. He ran across the bridge and moved along the bank, and a few moments later the lights of the cottage gleamed through the dark trees of the wood.

CHAPTER FOUR

It was cold in the stone-flagged kitchen and Jack Pope shivered involuntarily as he piled logs into the crook of one arm. He moved back along the passage and went into the living room of the small cottage.

Flames flickered across the oak-beamed ceiling, casting fantastic shadows that writhed and twisted convulsively and he piled more logs on to the already large fire.

He went to the dresser, took down a bottle of whisky and half filled a glass.

Outside the wind moaned, driving the rain against the window with the force of lead shot and he shivered, remembering the place on the other side of the hill beyond the river where he had spent five years of his life. He emptied the glass quickly, coughing as the raw spirit burned its way down his throat, and reached for the bottle again.

There was no sound, and yet a small cold wind touched him gently on the right cheek. He turned slowly, the hair rising on the nape of his neck.

Rogan stood in the doorway, shirt and pants plastered to his body, moulding his superb physique, rain mingling with the dust from the ventilating shafts, washing over him in a patina of filth.

And Jack Pope knew fear, real primeval fear that loosened the very bowels in him so that in the presence of this strange, dark man he was like a frightened child, completely dominated by some elemental force he couldn't even comprehend.

He moistened his dry lips and forced a ghastly smile. 'You made it, Irish. Good for you.'

Rogan crossed the room, soundlessly, took the glass from Pope's hand and poured the whisky down in one quick swallow. He closed his eyes, took a long breath and opened them again.

'What time is it?'

Pope glanced at his watch. 'Just after half past eight.'

'Good,' Rogan said. 'I want to be out of here by nine. Is there a bath?'

Pope nodded eagerly. 'I've had the water heating all afternoon.'

'Clothes?'

'Laid out in the bedroom. What about something to eat?'

Rogan shook his head. 'No time. If you've got a vacuum flask fill it with coffee and make a few sandwiches. I can eat them on the way.'

'Okay, Irish, anything you say. The bath's at the end of the passage.'

Rogan turned abruptly and went out, and immediately the forced smile was wiped from Pope's face. 'Who the hell does he think he is, the big stinking Mick. God, how I wish I could turn him in.'

He went into the kitchen, put the kettle on the stove, then he rummaged in a drawer till he found a bread-knife, took down a loaf and started viciously to cut it into slices.

The bathroom was a recent extension to the rear of the cottage and the bath itself was small. Not that it mattered. Rogan filled it with hot water, stripped off his wet clothes and climbed in. For a brief moment only he sat there enjoying the warmth, then he started to wash the filth from his body. Five minutes later, he stepped out, dried himself quickly, then went along the passage to the bedroom, a towel about his waist.

He found everything he needed laid out neatly across the bed. Underclothing, shirts, even the shoes were the right size and the two-piece suit in Glencarrick thornproof looked as if it had been made to measure. There was also a battered rain hat and an old trenchcoat. A nice touch that, he had to admit, however grudgingly. He took them with him when he returned to the living room.

Pope followed him in from the kitchen carrying a large vacuum flask and a tin biscuit box. 'Sandwiches are inside; it'll save you having to stop.'

'And just where am I supposed to be going?'

'O'More wants to see you.'

'Where do I find him?'

Pope shrugged. 'God knows. I've been working through an accommodation address in Kendal. Do you know where that is?'

'The Lake District, isn't it? Westmorland?'

'That's right. You're in for a long drive. It's all of three hundred and fifty miles from here and you've got to be there by seven in the morning.'

Which was the precise moment at which they would be turning out the cells at the prison and Rogan smiled slightly. They were hardly likely to be looking for him in a place like Kendal. It would take them at least three days to realize that he'd got off the moor and even then they wouldn't be sure.

'Why seven?'

'Because that's the time you're being picked up. You drive into the car park of the Woolpack Inn—that's in Stricklandgate—and wait.'

'Who for?'

'I honestly don't know. As I said, I've been writing to an accommodation address in Kendal. Maybe it's just a jumping off place to somewhere else.'

Rogan shook his head. 'Not good enough, Pope. You wouldn't go into anything blindfold.'

'It's the truth, Irish, as God's my judge. I'll admit I opened my mouth about that escape of yours when I got out and the word must have got around among the boys. You know how these things are.'

'What about Soames, the lawyer.'

'Been disbarred for the past five years. A villain down to the soles of his feet. He came to see me a couple of weeks ago. Said a client of his had heard this rumour about you having a way out and they'd traced it to me. It didn't take him long to get down to brass tacks. He's a downy bird.'

'And what's your cut?'

'For setting this little lot up? A couple of centuries and my expenses.'

Rogan helped himself to a cigarette from a packet on the table and lit it, an abstracted frown on his face. On the face of it, it didn't make sense—not any of it. And yet Colum was as cunning as a fox. It would be like him to cover his tracks again, making any direct route to him difficult to find.

'All right, for the moment, I'll buy it,' he said. 'How do I get to Kendal?'

Pope produced a small white folder and grinned. 'Nothing like being efficient, so I went to the top. Got you an A.A. route guide. It starts at Exeter and takes you straight through to Kendal.'

He went over it quickly, indicating the route on the excellent sketch maps provided. At Exeter Rogan would pick up the A38 and follow it through Bristol and Gloucester. From there, the new M5 motorway would take him north past Worcester and Birmingham, joining the M6 for the long run up through Lancashire to the Lake

District.

'You'll find some sections of the motorways are still under construction,' Pope said, 'but on the whole, you should have a pretty clear run.'

'What kind of car have you got for me?'

'Nothing special. A Ford brake, two years old but the engine's perfect. I've had it checked. You'll find a few samples of animal feed in the back. You're supposed to be a salesman for an agricultural firm.' He picked up a brief-case and produced various documents. 'Here's a couple of printed business cards in the name of Jack Mann and a driving licence. Hope you can still remember how.'

Rogan shrugged. 'I'll get by.'

There were insurance papers and log book, all in the same name. Even an Automobile Association member-ship card. Rogan tucked them all into his inside breast pocket.

'You seem to have thought of everything.'

'We aim to please.' Pope took out a worn leather wallet and passed it across. 'You'll find forty quid in there. No sense in carrying more. If you were stopped and searched it would only excite suspicion.'

'The police mind,' Rogan said. 'You can never get away from it, can you?'

Pope flushed, but managed to force a smile. 'That's about it.' He glanced at his watch. 'Almost nine. You'd better be on your way.'

Rogan pulled on the trenchcoat, belted it around his waist and picked up his hat. They went out through the kitchen and Pope flicked on an outside light, opened the door and led the way across the small courtyard to an old barn. He opened a large door, and two cars were re-vealed.

One of them was a large dark shooting brake, the other a green saloon. Rogan paused in the entrance, looking at them.

'Two?' he said.

'Well how in the hell do you think I'm going to get out

of here at this time of night?' Pope said. 'It was bad enough having to walk five miles to the nearest bus stop yesterday after driving out here in the Ford. I picked up the saloon in Plymouth this morning.'

Which was a good story had it not been for the fact that the wheels of both vehicles were still damp and muddy from the day's rain.

Rogan let it pass. 'I'd better be on my way.'

Pope nodded. 'Make sure it's the right one. No detours to Holyhead for the Irish boat.'

Rogan turned very slowly, his face quite expressionless. 'And what would you be meaning by that?'

Pope forced a smile. 'Nothing, Irish, nothing. It's just that the Big Man's invested a lot of money in you. He's entitled to see some return.'

The next moment, a hand had him by the throat, pulling him close and the rush of blood seemed to be forcing out his eyeballs.

'When I do a thing, it's because I want to,' Rogan said softly. 'Always remember that, Pope. Nobody crowds Sean Rogan.'

Pope went staggering back against the whitewashed wall and slumped to the ground. He crouched there, sobbing for breath, aware of the Ford starting up and moving out across the yard, the engine fading into the distance.

A footstep scraped on stone and a voice said calmly, 'Friend Rogan plays rough. A dangerous man to cross.'

Pope looked up at Henry Soames and cursed savagely. 'I hope you know what you're doing.' He groaned, swaying a little as he got to his feet. 'If I'd any sense I'd pull out of this now.'

'And lose out on all that lovely money?' Soames patted him on the shoulder. 'Let's go back inside and I'll go over it again. I think you'll see things my way.'

Round the bend of the road, Rogan parked the car by a five-barred gate and walked back the way he had come. There were several reasons for such a course. In the first place he didn't like Pope, in the second, he didn't trust him. And there was the intriguing fact that the tyres of both cars had been wet although the brake had supposedly been under cover since the previous day.

Nearing the cottage, he left the road, pushed his way through a plantation of damp fir trees and crossed the yard at the rear. A curtain was drawn across the window, but when he bent down he could see most of the living room through a narrow crack.

Henry Soames and Pope were sitting at the table engaged in earnest conversation, the whisky bottle between them. Rogan stayed there for only a moment, then turned and retraced his steps.

So—the plot thickened. Most puzzling thing of all, how did Colum O'More come to be mixed up with such people? There was no answer, could be none till he reached Kendal. He leaned back in his seat and concentrated on the road ahead.

CHAPTER FIVE

AFTER midnight Rogan had the road pretty much to himself, although from Bristol to Birmingham and north into Lancashire he came across plenty of heavy transport working the all-night routes.

Just after two a.m. he stopped at a small garage near Stoke to fill up, staying in the shadows of the car so that the attendant didn't get a clear look at his face.

He made good time, always keeping within any indicated speed limits, and dawn found him moving north along the M6 motorway east of Lancaster.

The morning was grey and sombre with heavy rain

clouds drifting across his path, and to the west the dark waters of Morecambe Bay were being whipped into whitecaps. He opened the side window and the wind carried the taste of good salt air and he inhaled deeply, feeling suddenly alive for the first time in years.

He stopped the car, took out the vacuum flask and stood at the side of the road looking out at the distant sea while he finished the coffee. It was difficult to believe, but he was out. For a brief moment, the strange, illogical thought crossed his mind that perhaps this was only some dark, hopeless dream from which the rattle of the key in the lock of his cell door would awaken him at any moment, and then a gull cried harshly in the sky and rain started to fall in a sudden heavy rush. He stood there for a moment longer, his face turned up to it, and then got back into the car and drove away.

He arrived in Kendal just after seven and found the place, like most country market towns at that time in the morning, already stirring. He located the Woolpack Inn in Stricklandgate without any trouble, pulled in the car park and switched off the engine.

It was a strange feeling waiting there in the car, like the old days working with the Maquis in France, and he remembered that morning in Amiens with the rain bouncing from the cobbles and the contact man who turned out to be an Abwehr agent. But then you never could be certain of anything in this life, from the womb to the grave.

He opened the packet of cigarettes Pope had given him, found it empty and crushed it in his hand. A quiet voice said, 'A fine morning, Mr. Rogan.'

She was perhaps twenty years old, certainly no more. She wore an old trenchcoat belted around her waist and, in spite of her headscarf, rain beaded the fringe of dark hair which had escaped at the front and drifted across her brow.

She walked round to the other side, opened the door and sat on the bench seat beside him. Her face was smoothly rounded with a flawless cream complexion, the eyebrows and hair coal black and her red lips had an extra fullness that suggested sensuality. It was the sort of face he had seen often on the west coast of Ireland, particularly around Galway where there had been a plentiful infusion of Spanish blood over the centuries.

'How could you be sure?' he said.

She shrugged. 'I had the number of the car and Colum showed me a photograph. You've changed.'

'Haven't we all?' he said. 'Where do you fit in?'

'You'll find out. If you'll let me get at that wheel, we'll move out.'

He eased himself across the seat. She slid past him. For a moment he was acutely conscious of her as a woman, a hint of perfume in the cold morning air, the edge of the coat riding above her knees. She pulled it down with a complete lack of self-consciousness and started the engine.

'I'd like to stop for some cigarettes,' Rogan said.

She took a packet from her left pocket and tossed them across. 'No need. I've got plenty.'

'Have we far to go?'

'About forty miles.'

She was perfectly calm, her hands steady on the wheel as she took the brake with real skill through the narrow streets and the early morning traffic, and he watched her for a while, leaning back in the corner.

A fine, lovely girl this one, but one who had been used by life and not kindly. The story was there in the shadow that lurked behind the grey-green eyes. Hurt, but not broken—the courage showed in the tilt of the chin, the sureness of those competent hands. The pity of it was that she would never let anyone get close to her again and that was the real tragedy.

Her voice cut sharply into his musing. 'You'll know me next time?'

'And would that be a bad thing?' he grinned lightly. 'Liverpool-Irish?'

'Is it that obvious?'

'No accent like it in this world or out of it.'

She smiled in spite of herself. 'You needn't think you sound like any English gentleman yourself.'

'And why would I be wanting to?'

'You were a major in their army, weren't you?'

'You seem to know.'

'I should do. At one time, I used to get the great Sean Rogan for breakfast, dinner and supper and precious little else.'

They were now on the outskirts of the town and she pulled in beside a low stone wall topped by iron railings. A little farther along there was an open iron gate and a sign which read *Church of the Immaculate Heart* with the times of Mass and Confession in faded gold letters beneath.

'Do you mind?' she said. 'I don't get in very often.'

'Suit yourself.'

He watched her pass through the gate, a small girl with a ripe peasant figure and hips that were too large by English standards. So, she still kept to the Faith? Now that was interesting, and proved she wasn't an active member of the I.R.A. which carried automatic excommunication.

On impulse he opened the door and followed her along the flagged path. It was warm inside and very quiet. For a little while he stood there listening intently and then he sat down in a pew at the back of the church.

She was on her knees by the altar. As he looked down towards the winking candles it seemed to grow darker. He leaned forward and rested his head on a stone pillar. All the strain and excitement of the past twelve hours catching up on him. In some strange way it was as if he were listening for something.

He pushed the thought away from him and sat back and watched as she got to her feet and walked back along the aisle. She became aware of him there in the half darkness and paused abruptly.

'That was foolish of you. You could have been seen.'

40

He shrugged, stood up and took her arm as they went to the door. 'If you think like that you act suspiciously; if you act suspiciously, you get caught. I'm an old hand at being on the run.'

They stood on the step and the wind blew a fine drizzle of rain into the porch as she looked up at him searchingly. She smiled and it was as if a lamp had been turned on inside.

'Hannah Costello, Mr. Rogan,' she said and held out her hand.

He took it and grinned. 'A fresh start makes old friends of bad ones,' he said. 'A proverb my grandmother was fond of. Would it be too much to ask where you're taking me?'

'The other side of the lakes. On the coast, near a place called Whitbeck.'

'Is Colum O'More there?'

'Waiting for you.'

'In the name of God, let us go then. There's a farm in Kerry my father's growing too old to cope with. It's time I was home again.'

The smile vanished from her face and she gazed up at him searchingly. She seemed about to speak, but obviously thought better of it and turned and led the way back to the car.

Dick Vanbrugh was tired, damned tired, and the heavy rain driving against the bathroom window wasn't calculated to improve the way he felt. He finished shaving and was towelling his face tenderly when the door opened and his wife looked in. 'Phone, darling. The Assistant Commissioner.'

Vanbrugh stared at her, a deep frown creasing his forehead. 'You're joking, of course.'

'I'm afraid not. I'll get your breakfast on the stove now. From the sound of him, you'll be moving off in a hurry.'

Vanbrugh pulled a shirt over his head, tucking it into

his trousers as he went downstairs. His tiredness had vanished completely. Whatever this was, it was something big. You didn't get the Assistant Commissioner on the phone at seven thirty in the morning just because somebody's warehouse had been turned over.

He picked up the phone from the hall stand and leaned against the wall. 'Vanbrugh here, sir.'

'Morning, Dick. I'm afraid I'm going to put you off your breakfast.'

'Not the first time,' Vanbrugh said.

'Rogan's out.'

Vanbrugh suddenly felt a little light-headed. He took a deep breath, closing his eyes and then opened them again.

'When?'

'Some time during the night. They found him missing at seven o'clock turn-out. The Governor's just been on the line to the Old Man.'

'How did he get out?'

'Nobody seems to know. They may come up with something later, but the first quick check disclosed nothing.'

Vanbrugh laughed gently. 'In the Maquis, they called him the Ghost, did you know that, sir?'

The Assistant Commissioner ignored the remark. 'You're in charge, Dick.'

Vanbrugh took a deep breath and stood up straight. 'I'd rather not—not this time.'

'He won't take no for an answer, Dick. After all, you know Rogan better than anyone else.'

'That's the trouble, sir.'

'There's a fast train for the West Country at nine from Paddington. Take Dwyer with you. I'll see that the local constabulary give you every co-operation. The longer he's out, the worse it will be. The newsboys will start digging up his war record and so on and before you know where you are, we'll be in it right up to our necks.'

'Would that be such a bad thing, sir?' Vanbrugh said.

42

'It might make the Home Secretary think again if nothing else.'

'Respond to this kind of emotional blackmail? You must be mad.' The Assistant Commissioner snorted. 'For God's sake try to remember you're a copper and get moving.'

Vanbrugh replaced the receiver, stood there thinking for a moment, then put through a quick call to Detective Sergeant Dwyer at his home. When he was finished, he went into the kitchen. His wife turned from the stove, a frying pan in her hand, and he shook his head.

'Just coffee, love. I've got to get moving.'

She filled his cup, placed it on the table before him, then ran her fingers through his greying hair. 'Twenty-five years, Dick. I should know you by now. What's gone wrong?'

'It's Sean,' he said. 'Sean Rogan. He's on the loose. The Old Man wants me to go down to the West Country to take charge of the hunt personally.'

'Oh, no, Dick.' A spasm of pain crossed her face and she sank into the opposite chair. 'Haven't you done enough?'

'I'm a policeman, Nell,' he said. 'You knew it when you married me. Sean knew.'

'But, Dick, he saved your life.'

'God in Heaven, do you think I don't know that?' he demanded.

When she put out her hand and gently touched his face there were tears in her eyes. He turned the hand and brushed his lips against the palm.

'I'd better get moving, love. I haven't got much time.'

He got to his feet, turned and went out slowly.

It was still raining when Rogan and the girl reached Bowness and took the ferry across Lake Windermere. The boat was deserted and they stood at the stern rail taking in the beauty.

'What do you think of it?' she said.

'It's certainly spectacular.'

43

'The most beautiful place in England. In the summer these roads are crowded with holidaymakers. At this time of the year, you won't see a soul. That's when I like it best.'

There was a glow to her cheeks and she wiped moisture away from her brow carelessly and looked across at Belle Isle. Rogan watched her, aware of beauty and gladdened by it.

On the other side, they took the road to Hawkshead, then turned down the far side of Coniston Water to Broughton-in-Furness and Whicham. From there, they turned north along the coast road and a mile beyond Whitbeck Station they came to a signpost carrying the legend, Marsh-End. She turned off the road and bumped over a rutted track towards the sea.

They followed the course of a winding creek that twisted like a snake, losing itself in a country of rough grass marshes and mud flats where wild ducks nested in the reeds and fog drifted in from the sea, dulling the edges of things so that they lacked definition, formless as in a dream.

The brake turned into another track which led through a clump of fir trees, and on the other side a lonely farmhouse stood at the head of a creek.

It stood in a clump of beech trees at the water's edge, an ancient grey-stone building with a good barn and a walled yard. It was only as they approached that Rogan became aware of the decay that hung over everything, of the broken fences, peeling paintwork.

Grass grew between the cobbles, and as the car rolled to a halt Hannah Costello switched off the engine and grimaced.

'Not much of a place. Over the years, the tides have eroded all the pasture. No one could make a living here except by wildfowling and fishing. The agents were glad to lease it for a year.'

He frowned. 'A long time.'

'Anything less would have looked suspicious.'

44

She hesitated and then went on, 'How long is it since you last saw Colum O'More?'

'Ten years.'

'You'll find him changed. Try not to show it. I think his pride means a lot to him.'

Before Rogan could reply, the door behind him opened and he turned quickly. The man who stood there leaned heavily on a stick, head slightly forward from great hunched shoulders.

'Sean,' he said in a hoarse whisper. 'Sean Rogan, by all that's holy.'

The shock was like a physical blow and Rogan swallowed hard and moved to meet him, hand outstretched. 'Colum, you old devil. A long time.'

For a moment in their handclasp there was a touch of the old strength he remembered, but only for a moment and Colum O'More laughed harshly. 'They say Time changes all things, Sean. Me, he decided to kick straight in the teeth. I'm glad he's dealt better by you.'

He turned and limped along the whitewashed corridor and Rogan followed him, aware of the clothes hanging in folds upon the skeleton of the man he had once known.

The living room was simply furnished with a table, a couple of easy chairs by the fire on the open hearth and rush matting on the floor. Colum O'More sank into one of the chairs and looked at Hannah.

'There's a bottle on the sideboard, girl, and glasses, and don't be telling me I shouldn't. I'm past caring.'

Rogan unbelted his coat, took it off and sat in the other chair. 'What happened, Colum?'

The old man shrugged. 'The hard life I've led, past sins catching up on me. Does it matter?' He shook his head. 'I've never seen a man look better from seven years in an English gaol.'

Rogan shrugged. 'Remember what Tom Clarke wrote? Never give in. Keep fighting and hang on to your self-respect?'

O'More nodded. 'And didn't he do just that for fifteen years?'

Hannah poured whisky into two glasses and brought them across and the old man slipped an arm around her waist. 'Lucky for her I'm not thirty years younger, Sean. A hundred per cent this one.' He smiled up at her. 'Make him some breakfast, girl, while we talk.'

She looked once at Rogan, an unspoken message in her eyes, and went out. O'More drank some of his whisky and sighed with pleasure. He took out a pipe and started to fill it from a worn leather pouch. 'You've just been on the news. By now they'll be running round in circles blocking every road off that damned moor and here you are, three hundred and fifty miles away where they'd least expect to find you. There must be a small laugh in that, surely.'

Rogan toasted him briefly. 'Thanks to the Big Man.'

'The Organization looks after its own,' Colum O'More said. 'The time we've taken, I'll admit, but that was no fault of mine.'

There was a small silence and Rogan said carefully, 'And what would be the quickest way to Kerry from here, Colum?'

'Well, now, Sean, wasn't it that I wanted to discuss with you?'

There was something deep here, something he as yet didn't understand, that had been under the surface of things since Soames had made his visit to the prison a hundred years ago. Rogan took out a cigarette and lit it with a burning splinter from the fire.

'It's been a long time, Colum, too long for awkwardness between us. Say what you have to say.'

The old man shrugged. 'It's simply told. We have a job for you.'

'We?'

'The Organization.'

'I understood it had folded when they called off the border war.'

46

Colum O'More chuckled. 'A tale for fools and old women, but times have been difficult, Sean. We're re-organizing on a big scale, we need money.'

'And where would we be finding that?'

The old man turned to the table, opened the drawer and took out a map which he unfolded on the floor. It showed the Lake District in detail and he used his stick as a pointer.

'The Glasgow to London mail train comes down through Carlisle and Penrith. Notice that it doesn't touch Kendal. That's served by a local line. It joins the main line at Rigg Station eight miles south of Kendal.'

'So?'

'Every Friday, the Central Banks Association sends an armoured van from Penrith. It does a sort of circle through the Lakes and down the coast, calling at Keswick, Whitehaven, Seascale and so on. From Broughton, which you'll have passed through on your way here, it goes up to Ambleside, then down through Windermere to Kendal. It arrives at Rigg Station at three in the afternoon where it meets up with the London Express.'

'What kind of stuff do they carry?'

'The usual weekend cash surplus, mainly old notes for re-pulping. You know what the banks are like. They don't like it lying around these country branches. Usually around a quarter of a million.'

'A useful sum.'

'It would be to the Organization.'

Rogan laughed harshly. 'God save us all, but here's madness for you!' He paced across to the window, then swung round angrily. 'Was it for this you helped me out after seven years, Colum O'More?'

'You're the best brain we ever had,' O'More said calmly, 'the best organizer. We needed you.'

'And if you hadn't, where would I be now, Colum O'More?'

'It took a lot to get you out, lad, and not only in hard cash. I'm depending on you.'

'Then you'll be disappointed.' Rogan shook his head and moved back to the fireside. 'I've had it up to here, Colum, can't you see that? Forty years old and I've spent twelve of them in gaol. As far as I'm concerned, the game's played out. The Organization must find another way to get what it wants. I've had my bellyful.'

The old man nodded. 'And what will you be doing?'

'There's a farm in Kerry waiting for me now, you know that as well as I do. My father's been running it since he retired from the political service ten years ago. He's getting old, Colum, and so am I.'

'Aren't we all?' The old man sighed. 'So be it. North of here there's a place on the coast called Ravenglass. I'll give you the name of a man I know. He'll see you across the water for a hundred pounds.' He opened the drawer again, took out a packet of banknotes and tossed them on the table. 'Good luck to ye, Sean Rogan.'

Rogan picked up the notes, weighing them in his hand, a frown on his face. 'And you?'

'God save us, lad, I've a job to do and men waiting ready for it back there in those mountains. I'll see this thing through on my own.'

Rogan stood staring at him for a moment, then he turned without a word, flung open the door and moved outside.

CHAPTER SIX

The tide was drifting in, gurgling in crab holes, stippled water covering the mud-flats with an expanse of shining silver that moved among sea asters, and somewhere a curlew cried, lonely in a sombre world.

Rogan crossed a narrow stone causeway and followed a path through rough marsh grass and reeds that were head high. On impulse he took an even narrower path to the right and, pushing his way through the undergrowth, emerged at the side of a narrow creek and found a motor launch moored to the bank.

There was no sign of life and he jumped down on to the deck and moved into the wheelhouse. Although the boat was obviously old, it was in good condition and the interior had recently been swept. The brass compass mounting and engine controls were brightly polished. There was a movement out on the deck behind him and he turned to see Hannah Costello standing watching him.

He moved out to join her and she tossed his trenchcoat across. 'I thought you might need this.'

He pulled it on, turning up the collar against the rain, and lit another cigarette. 'Is this Colum's?'

She nodded. 'He sailed it down from Ravenglass himself.'

'His quick exit when the job's done?' She nodded and he shook his head. 'Well not me, I'm moving out now.'

'No one's stopping you.'

With a sudden rush the rain increased into a solid downpour and he stared out across the marsh. 'A strange place this, like nowhere I've ever been. You'd swear there were eyes watching you from every thicket.'

'Spirits of the dead,' she said. 'This is an ancient place. Ravenglass was a port even in Roman times. They called it Glannaventa. Not much more than a hundred years ago they found a longboat aground on the mud-flats at dawn half-filled with blood and a dozen revenuers with their throats cut. The free-traders used the farmhouse as their headquarters.'

'Nothing changes,' he said.

She nodded. 'The hardest lesson to learn. All my life I've been trying to change things, change me even. I always end up back at base.'

'How do you fit into all this?'

'That's an easy one. I live with my uncle, Paddy Costello, at a place called Scardale, in the fells north of Ambleside. He has an excuse for a sheep farm up there that's just about on its last legs. He and my father were members of the Big Man's Organization in the North of England during the war. He found out about this bank van six months ago and got in touch with Colum.'

'Why should he do that?'

'Because drunk or sober—which isn't often—he lives in a dream world of action and passion and God Save Ireland, cried the heroes. He sees himself still one of them carrying on the gallant struggle.'

'And is that such a bad thing?'

'It's a foolish dream,' she said, 'which is worse. An echo of something that's gone for ever. The world's changed and it doesn't need men like my uncle any longer.'

'Or me?'

'If the cap fits. Are you going to take that boat out of Ravenglass?'

'I'd be a fool if I didn't.'

She leaned against the rail and stared back into the past. 'When I was a kid in Liverpool, all I ever got was Sean Rogan—the great Sean Rogan. My old man was by way of being a fan of yours. At least that's what he said loudly across every bar counter on the waterfront. But that's as far as it ever went. After my mother died, the drinking really got a hold on him.'

'I've seen it happen,' Rogan said. 'A bad thing.'

'Funny how someone can destroy themselves in front of you,' she said. 'Even your love for them. I didn't end up hating him, I just didn't care. When he started mistaking my bedroom for his when he staggered in, I thought it was time to move on. He died the following year.'

'What did you do?'

'What every girl in my position does—went to London.'

'How old were you?'

'Sixteen, but that turned out to be a distinct advantage. Girls of that age have a strong appeal for some men.'

'So I've heard,' he said gravely.

'I got a job as a waitress, but that wouldn't keep me in room and board. Then one of the customers offered me a job in his club. I was always a good dancer.' She smiled calmly. 'They're right when they go on about the importance of the little sins—the Church, I mean. It's amazing how quickly you can become what you never thought you would.'

'It sounds like a bad plot.'

'It gets even better. The police moved in and it turned out the boss had been squeezing some of the more respectable customers dry on the side. He dragged three of us down with him.'

'What did you get?'

'Six months. When I got out, I wrote to Uncle Paddy. His wife had died and he needed a woman round the place. He's got a son, Brendan, aged seventeen. Had meningitis when he was a kid.' She touched her head. 'Needs looking after.'

'And now you're up to your ears in this lot? Why don't you just pack your bags and get out?'

She shrugged, and watched the mist creeping in from the sea. 'Why does anybody do anything? You become involved, I suppose, just like a fish in a net. Choose which way you twist, there's no way out.' She looked up at him, her face quite calm. 'That's how I've been all my life, Mr. Rogan, trapped in an invisible net with no way out.'

There was a stillness about her, a strange, brooding calm, and the green eyes held his steadily. It was as if she wanted him to say something, perhaps offer some solution, but there was nothing of value he could say.

'I've been trying to crash out of something all my life and I'm forty years old.'

She nodded slowly. 'I think you are a man held too easily by old loyalties.'

Which was a remarkably shrewd observation and Rogan lit another cigarette and changed the subject. 'What kind of a set-up has Colum got back there in the mountains?'

'At Scardale? Nothing very complicated. He's recruited a couple of tearaways from Manchester. Professional crooks, they've been there a week now.'

'What are they like?'

'Smash their way in, smash their way out and God help anyone who gets in the way. You know the type. Only one of them is really dangerous. That's Morgan—Harry Morgan. He's got brains of a sort. Fletcher's just a blunt instrument.'

'Nice people Colum O'More's got himself mixed up with.'

She shrugged. 'For this kind of a job, you need experts and Morgan and Fletcher are that all right.'

'How did he get in touch with them?'

'I think Soames found them for him.'

'Have you ever met him?'

She shook her head. 'Colum has, but only once. That was in Liverpool. Since then, we've used an accommodation address—a back-street newsagent's in Kendal. I've usually collected the letters by hand.'

'So Soames doesn't know about this place?'

'Marsh-End?' She shook her head. 'Even my uncle hasn't been here. Morgan's tried following me a few times, but I've always given him the slip.'

'There was a man called Pope—Jack Pope. He was waiting for me when I got out. Where does he fit in?'

'As far as I know, he was paid to do a particular job and that was an end to it. Soames handled all the negotiations at that end.'

'How much was Soames paid?'

'Five hundred and his expenses.'

Rogan shook his head. 'Not enough. His kind live under stones. He'll want more.'

She frowned. 'How could he get it?'

'I don't know, but he and Pope are up to something and whatever it is, it isn't going to do Colum any good.' He flipped his cigarette down into the water. 'Come on, let's get back.'

She caught his sleeve and held him a moment. 'What are you going to do?'

'God knows, but he's an old man. I can't let him put his head on the block without doing something about it, now can I?'

He turned, scrambled over the rail and pushed his way through the wet undergrowth back towards the farmhouse.

Colum O'More sat at the table, a large scale map of the Lake District in front of him. When the door clicked open behind him, he didn't bother to move and Rogan sat on the edge of the table.

He looked down at the map, a slight frown on his face. 'One thing I don't understand, Colum? Why you? Where are the young and active ones? Safe in their beds?'

The old man shrugged. 'I first heard about this bank van through an old comrade, Paddy Costello. Hannah's uncle.'

'She told me about him.'

'I put the idea before the headquarters staff in Waterford. They said it couldn't be done. That it was too risky.' He chuckled harshly. 'I thought I'd show them there was life in the old dog yet.'

'The money that got me out,' Rogan said. 'Where did that come from?'

'Does it matter?'

'It might.'

Colum O'More shrugged. 'I had some savings. That and a mortgage on my house in Lismore.'

Rogan shook his head. 'No fool like an old one.'

'Oh, don't be worrying about me. I'll get my expenses paid out of the proceeds of this one.'

Rogan shook his head. 'It won't work, Colum. You're

too old.'

The old man went very white, eyes like hot coals. The stick swung up as if he would strike Rogan across the face with it and then a spasm of pain racked his face. He clapped a hand to his mouth too late and a quantity of brown vomit erupted, spilling across the stone floor.

There was a quick exclamation from the doorway and when Rogan turned, Hannah was standing there. 'A cloth,' he said, 'and some water. Quickly now.'

He held the old man's head up until the girl came back. She gently swabbed away the vomit with a damp cloth and Rogan took his arm and pulled him up.

'He'll be better lying down.'

The bedroom was on the ground floor at the rear, and he sat the old man on the edge of the bed, took off his jacket and loosened his collar. Colum O'More lay back with a sigh and Rogan raised his feet and threw a coverlet over him.

He walked with the girl to the door. 'Have you seen him like this before?'

She nodded. 'Once. It was exactly the same. He was all right again within half an hour.'

There was a ghostly chuckle from the bed and when Rogan turned, O'More was looking at him through half open eyes. 'I received my sentence from the finest physician in Dublin three months ago, lad. A couple of years, maybe three and there's an end of it.'

Rogan stood at the side of the bed looking down at him. 'Will you be all right?'

'Fine. Right as a trivet in half an hour. I've had these attacks before.'

'Good,' Rogan said. 'Just take it easy then and don't worry about a thing.'

When he closed the door, the girl was standing in the passage, a puzzled frown on her face. 'Why—I don't understand?'

He could have talked to her of old loyalties, of what he owed to a man whose proud boast had been that he had never let a friend down in his life come hell or high water. But the thing went deeper than that.

From the moment he had dropped over the wall back there on the moor, he had been caught in a current from which there was no escaping until he reached the pre-ordained end.

That was the Celt in him speaking and still a poor reason.

'Make him a cup of tea and lace it with whisky. I'll sit with him for a while.'

He pushed her along the passage, opened the bedroom door and went back inside. He sat on the edge of the bed, took out his cigarettes and lit one slowly.

'All right,' he said to O'More. 'I want the lot. Places, names, who does what and when.'

'You'll do it, Sean?' the old man said eagerly. 'You'll handle it for me?'

'I'll look into it,' Rogan said. 'I'll go to Costello's place and I'll take a look at the set-up. More than that I won't promise.'

Colum O'More's breath was exhaled in a long sigh. 'And that's good enough for me.'

CHAPTER SEVEN

HARRY MORGAN came awake and stared up at the stained and peeling ceiling. Looked at long enough, it became a pretty fair map of London, and he recalled with nostalgia a little bar off Dean Street in Soho that had been a favourite haunt of his in the old days, and the Greek girl who ran it. Now there was a woman ...

His throat was dry and his mouth tasted bad. He

pushed himself up on one elbow and groped under the bed until he located a bottle. It was empty and he dropped it to the floor and stood up, a lean dark man with red hair, black eyes and a mouth that curled sardonically at the corners.

He pulled an old sweater over his head and moved to the door outside; then there was a howl of rage. As Morgan opened the door and moved into the whitewashed passage, Costello's half-witted son, his mouth gaping in fear, stumbled into him, Fletcher hard on his heels.

Fletcher, a great ox of a man, grabbed for the boy and Morgan barred his way with an outstretched arm. 'Now what?'

'The bloody little swine's pinched all my fags. There were three packets under my pillow. They've all gone.'

'You lost them to me at brag last night,' Morgan said. 'You were too damned drunk to remember.'

'You can stick that for a tale.'

Fletcher pushed him roughly to one side and grabbed at the boy, who ran to the end of the passage and pulled open the door. What happened next was so quick and confusing, that afterwards Fletcher had difficulty in recalling the incident clearly.

One moment he was reaching for the scruff of the boy's neck, the next he was stumbling headlong to the cobbles of the yard. He started to turn and a foot pushed down hard across his throat. Fletcher began to choke and then the pressure was relieved. When he managed to control his breathing again, he found himself looking up into a hard, implacable face.

Jesse Fletcher had never been afraid of anything or anybody in his entire life and he felt no fear now, only the natural wariness of a born fighting man who senses the same qualities in another.

'Get up!' Sean Rogan said.

Behind him, Hannah Costello stood by the brake, an arm around the boy's shoulders and Morgan laughed gently from the doorway. 'A touching scene.' He came forward as Fletcher scrambled to his feet. 'I'm Harry Morgan, Mr. Rogan, and this relic of a more primeval time is Jesse Fletcher. You'll have to excuse his lack of manners. They weren't handing out brains the day he was born.'

'One of these days I'll fill that big mouth of yours full of dirt,' Fletcher said viciously and turned and went inside.

'Where's my uncle?' Hannah demanded.

'He went into Ambleside in the truck for supplies. I'll be surprised if we see him back before the pubs close.'

He stood to one side with a slight, mocking grin and Rogan moved past him into the house. When he went into the large, stone flagged living room, Fletcher was sitting in a chair by the window, a bottle in one hand, a glass in the other.

Rogan ignored him and turned as Hannah and Morgan followed him in. 'Where's the boy?'

'Taken himself off into the hills,' she said. 'He won't be back till dark. He often does that.'

'What about beds?'

'There are two rooms upstairs. I've got one, my uncle and Brendan share another.'

'Jesse and I are across the passage,' Morgan said.

Fletcher snorted. 'Maybe he'd like us to move out?'

Rogan looked at him calmly. 'When I do, I'll let you know.'

He brushed past Morgan and followed Hannah along to the kitchen. Fletcher swallowed his whisky with a curse. 'The great Sean Rogan—what a laugh. Just a big Irish bogtrotter. One belt in the right place and he'd split clear down the middle.'

'Why don't you tell him that, Jesse?'

'Maybe I'll do just that.'

Morgan chuckled. 'Let me know when, I'd like to be there.'

In the kitchen, Rogan sat on the edge of the table and

lit a cigarette, and Hannah took off her coat and hung it behind the door. 'Ham and eggs all right?'

'Fine,' he said and walked to the window.

The wind rushed through the old beech trees which encircled the place, plucking most of the remaining leaves from the branches and lifting them high over the roof top, and his eyes lifted to the heather-covered hill-side and the mountains beyond.

'Quite a place. Anyone ever come here?'

'Only a few fell walkers or climbers and we see them mostly during spring and summer. The road peters out a quarter of a mile from here. A hundred and fifty years ago they mined for lead up there till the vein ran out. You can still see the old workings. Brendan can tell you all about that.'

'He seemed a nice enough kid.'

She nodded. 'A bit slower than other people, that's all. Uncle Paddy treats him like a dog, that's a lot of the trouble.'

'A sweet bunch Colum's surrounded himself with.'

'What did you think of the two in there?'

'Fletcher's just a second rate tearaway. A good man in a clinch with an iron bar or at putting in the boot. Morgan's a different proposition. For one thing he's got brains.'

'Don't let that fool you,' she said. 'Fletcher I can understand. He's too ignorant to be anything else, but Morgan's bad because he wants to be. You'll have to watch him. His favourite occupation seems to be stirring up trouble, then standing back to watch the fun.'

'The best way I know to burn your fingers,' Rogan said. 'Someone should tell him.'

She placed ham and eggs before him and a plate piled high with fresh bread and butter and sat on the other side of the table, a cup of tea in her hands, and watched him eat.

'You needed that,' she observed when he finally pushed the empty plate away with a sigh.

He smiled slightly. 'And not because I was hungry. I'm the great one for symbolic actions. Not that they fed us too badly in there. It's just that it tastes different on the outside.'

They lit cigarettes and sat there smoking in a companionable silence, rain tapping lightly against the window, and after a while Morgan came in and found them there. He took a cup, helped himself to tea from the pot and sat on the edge of the dresser.

'How was O'More?'

'In good shape,' Rogan said.

Morgan laughed harshly. 'No need to keep that up with me, big man. When Jesse and I met him in Manchester a couple of weeks back it was taking him all his time to stay on his feet.'

'So?'

'The way I see it he's on the way out. It takes a good man to run a thing like this, a strong man.'

'I know,' Rogan said softly. 'That's why I'm here.'

'Who the hell says so?' Jesse Fletcher filled the doorway, the ugly scarred face flushed in anger. 'Who says we even need you? Maybe Morgan and me got our own plans.'

'O'More told me you were working for wages,' Rogan said. 'Five grand apiece. Right?'

'That's what the contract says.'

'Then tell the hired help here to shut his big mouth.'

Fletcher took a convulsive step forward and Morgan said sharply, 'Hold your fire, Jesse, fighting among ourselves won't get us anywhere.' He turned to Rogan and shrugged. 'Jesse gets annoyed easily. It's understandable. Since that one meeting in Manchester we haven't clapped eyes on O'More. Hannah is the only link we've got with him. Even her uncle doesn't know where he's staying.'

'Caution's his second name,' Rogan said. 'No harm in that. You'll see him at the right time.' He stood up. 'What about this plan of yours?'

'I've got a map in the sitting room,' Morgan said. 'Let's

go through.'

Outside the rain had stopped and the sky had cleared a little over the mountains as evening fell. It was dark in the living room, shadows gathering in the corners, and Hannah lit an oil lamp and placed it in the centre of the old mahogany table. Morgan took a large scale map of the area from a drawer and unfolded it.

'Here's Scardale,' he said. 'Five miles north of Ambleside below Scardale Fell. Ambleside to Windermere, five miles, then straight into Kendal. Rigg Station's five miles south.'

'About twenty-five miles in all.'

'That's it. Rigg's only a way station. The sort of place that has a stationmaster-cum-porter. Busy during the season when all the holiday trains pass through to the Lake District. Like a grave at this time of the year.'

'What about this Friday afternoon mail train? Can a passenger board it at Rigg?'

Morgan shook his head. 'It isn't a scheduled stop any more. The railways have been doing a lot of reorganization during the past couple of years and Rigg Station's just the sort of place where the axe has fallen. In fact the stationmaster, if you can call him that, is more of a caretaker than anything else. He doesn't even live on the premises any more. Comes out from Kendal each day.'

'What about the armoured van? From what Colum said, it sounds like a tough nut to crack.'

'Just a bloody great steel box on wheels, the sort of thing the Central Banks are using all the time these days, and they've got a radio telephone hook-up to County Police Headquarters. They call in every half hour.'

'Where's the weak link, Rigg Station?'

Morgan shook his head. 'The van never arrives more than five minutes before the train. There's an unloading ramp at the side of the station and they back up to it and sit tight till the train comes.'

'You're sure about that?'

'Ask Hannah. She sat outside in the car the other

60

Friday and the week before that, Fletcher and I saw everything through glasses from a wood on the hillside. If you're thinking about taking them there, forget it. There wouldn't be time and the train's got a radio telephone as well. They all have since someone took them for a couple of million the other year.'

'A tough one.'

Morgan nodded. 'The old man seemed to think we could simply ambush the van on a quiet stretch of the road between Rigg and Kendal which shows you how much he's behind the times.'

'And you have a better idea?'

Fletcher laughed harshly. 'The best thing you ever heard of, Jack. Go on, tell him, Harry.'

'We've got an old Morris van out in the barn,' Morgan said. 'Now the way I see it, only one thing would tempt those two guards to break the rules and get out of their van—a bad road accident.'

'And you intend to provide one?'

'That's it. There's a good place about two miles out of Rigg Station. We've checked it half a dozen times. Only the occasional farm truck uses the road. At the right moment, we heave the old van over on its side, spill a little petrol and set it on fire. Even better, one of us lies in the road with blood on his face. They're bound to stop for that. No man on earth would go driving by.'

'Which is when the rest move in?'

Morgan nodded. 'Simple, isn't it?'

'Too simple.'

Rogan glanced across at Hannah, who returned his gaze calmly, no expression on her face and Fletcher said, 'You've got something better, I suppose?'

'Not yet,' Rogan said, 'but one thing's certain. It couldn't be any worse.' Morgan's lips tightened in anger, but Rogan carried on, 'There are two king-size flaws. In the first place the moment they come across the crash, the van guards will contact County Police Headquarters. They're bound to do that every time something out of the ordinary happens. You'd have a car on its way from Kendal within five minutes, and they'd expect another message from the armoured van, the moment the crash had been investigated. If they didn't get one, they'd turn the county out.'

What he had said was so obviously true that Fletcher and Morgan were reduced to silence, but Rogan carried relentlessly on. 'Even if we assume that I'm completely wrong, that the van guards are so upset at the sight of the crash, that they don't bother contacting police head-quarters, you still have the situation at Rigg Station to consider. What happens when the van fails to show? You said yourself that all mail trains carry radio telephones now. The first thing the guard will do will be to contact the proper authorities to notify them that the van hasn't shown up. Within minutes, the whole county would be buzzing like a hive of bees. They'll have a master plan ready for this sort of thing—they always do.'

Hannah laughed somewhere deep down in her throat and Fletcher turned angrily. 'You keep your mouth shut.'

Morgan put a hand on his arm and shook his head. 'No, he's right, Jesse. Every damned thing he says makes sense.' He looked across at Rogan, his eyes dark shadows in the lamplight. 'You've got something better?'

'There's always something better if only you can find it,' Rogan said. 'I'll look the situation over in the morning.'

At that moment, an old, high-sided cattle truck turned in through the gate, one battered wing scraping the stone post, and bumped across the cobblestones. It halted a foot from the wall of the house, the door swung open and an old man almost fell out.

He walked past the window, swaying from side to side and Morgan shook his head in disgust. 'In and out of every boozer in Ambleside shooting off his big mouth and spending money like water.'

'And no affair of yours if he does,' Hannah said, an angry red spot in each cheek.

The outer door opened and a rich, fruity voice broke into song:

God save Ireland, cried the heroes,
God save Ireland, cry we all,
Whether on the scaffold high or the battlefield we die,
Sure no matter when for Ireland dear we fall.

He paused in the doorway, a stupid grin on his blotched whisky face. 'God save all here.'

There was a slight pregnant silence and then Rogan said calmly, 'God save you kindly.'

The mouth gaped in the old man's face and he stared fixedly at Rogan. 'Holy Mother of God,' he said in a whisper. He staggered across the room and seized Rogan's hand. 'The great day this is for me, Mr. Rogan. The great day.'

He blinked his rheumy eyes several times and Rogan wrinkled his nose in disgust at the stale, beery smell that surrounded him.

'You've been into Ambleside?' he said.

'I have indeed, Mr. Rogan. A little matter of business connected with the farm.'

'Did you hear anything about me?'

The old man took a folded evening newspaper from his pocket and passed it across. 'There's an item at the bottom of the second page.'

It was no more than half a dozen lines. A brief mention of his escape and the fact that every exit from the moor had been blocked. There was no photo.

Rogan tossed the paper on to the table and turned back to Costello. 'You don't go into Ambleside again, or anywhere else for that matter unless I give you permission. Understand?'

'Oh, I do, Mr. Rogan. I do indeed.'

'And that goes for the rest of you.'

He left the room, went along the passage and stood by the cattle truck looking across the yard and down the valley towards Ambleside. Lake Windermere was a distant flash of silver in the dusk, and on either hand the mountains lifted steeply. There was the scrape of a shoe behind and he turned to see Fletcher and Morgan in the doorway.

'The girl tells me the road peters out a quarter of a mile up the valley?'

Morgan nodded. 'There's a few broken-down cottages up there and an old lead mine. The sort of place that gives you the creeps. I've only been up there once.'

Rogan looked down the valley again at the dirt road white in the gloaming. 'One way in and one way out. That doesn't sound too healthy.'

'You're telling us,' Fletcher said. 'Half a dozen scuffers down there with a couple of cars across the road and we've had it. Christ knows why O'More had to pick a place like this.'

'Because anywhere else, you two would have stuck out like a couple of sore thumbs,' Rogan said and walked away across the yard to the gate.

The two men watched him turn into the road and climb the slope towards the head of the valley and Fletcher spat viciously. 'God, how I'd like to cut that bastard down to size.'

'Never mind that,' Morgan said. 'We've got more important things to think of.'

They went back into the living room and found Costello in a chair by the fire, a glass of whisky in his hand. 'Where's the girl?' Morgan demanded.

'Making me a sandwich in the kitchen.'

'Did you see Pope?'

The old man nodded. 'He's staying at a small hotel just outside Ambleside—The White Grange. I told him you'd ring him some time tomorrow.'

'And how in the hell do I do that?'

'There's a public call box at the bottom of the valley where the track joins the main road.'

Morgan sat on the edge of the table, a frown on his

face, then turned and looked down at the map. 'I'd like to know what Rogan intends to do.'

'He won't know that himself till he's looked things over,' Fletcher said.

Morgan shook his head. 'I wouldn't be too sure. He's got it up here, that one.' He tapped his forehead. 'He's thought of something already, I could tell.'

'Then sooner or later, he's got to tell us what it is,' Costello said. 'He can't pull the job on his own.'

He laughed foolishly, whisky dribbling from the corner of his mouth and Morgan grabbed him by the tie, pulling him up from his chair. 'You'd better lay off that stuff, Dad. You're beginning to make me nervous. Just remember you're in this with the rest of us right up to your chin, and Rogan's no fool. The slightest slip from any of us and he'll smell a king-sized rat and a minimum of fifty thousand quid each is too much to lose because an old soak like you can't keep off the booze.'

A draught touched him lightly on the face and he turned and saw Hannah standing in the doorway, a tray in her hands. She moved in, her face expressionless and placed the tray on the table.

'You keep on sneaking around as quietly as that and we'll have to put a bell on you,' Morgan said.

She ignored him and spoke to her uncle. 'Coffee and sandwiches. If you want any more you'll have to get them yourself.'

She left the room, and a moment later they saw her pass the window and cross the yard to the gate. 'Do you think she heard anything?' Fletcher said.

Morgan frowned. 'One thing's for sure. We'll have to keep an eye on her. I don't like the way she looks at that big Mick.'

'Do me a favour,' Fletcher said. 'He's twice her age.'

Morgan shook his head pityingly. 'You know, there are times when you amaze me, Jesse, you really do.'

He turned, slapped the old man's hand as he reached for a sandwich and started to eat them himself.

On the slope above the farm, Rogan sat on a stone and lit a cigarette. In the far distance, Lake Windermere cut into the heart of the hills, black with depth near the centre, purple and grey at the edges. In the desolate light of gloaming, the tops of the mountains were streaked with orange.

The beauty of it was too much for a man and he breathed deeply on the sweetness of the heather, damp from the day's rain, filled with pleasant nostalgia.

'It's quite a view, isn't it?' Hannah Costello said.

He turned and found her standing a few yards away, watching him. 'I didn't hear a thing,' he said. 'I must be getting old.'

He took out his cigarettes and offered her one, and when she bent her face to the match which flared in his cupped hands her eyes were fathomless, so deep a man might drown in them.

She sat on the tilted slab of stone beside him and blew out a plume of smoke. 'There's something going on down there.'

'Between Morgan and Fletcher?'

'My uncle, too. They were arguing together. I heard them from the passage. Something about this man Pope, the one who was waiting for you when you got out. He's in Ambleside now.' Rogan nodded and she frowned. 'You don't seem surprised?'

'I'm not.' He told her about Jack Pope and Soames and of how he had seen them together on his return to the cottage on the moor. 'What else did they say?'

'Morgan's phoning him tomorrow from the call box on the main road. I suppose he'll wait to hear your verdict on the job.'

'That's about the size of it.'

'Another thing. He was talking about fifty thousand pound shares. I thought they were supposed to be getting five thousand each?'

'It looks as though Morgan intends to cut the cake differently.'

66

'You still don't look worried.'

'It'll work out, you'll see.' He smiled warmly. 'It's nice to know someone's on my side, anyway.'

She flushed perceptibly and he looked over the valley into the dark arch of the sky where a single star shone. For several minutes they sat there in silence and then she said softly, 'What are you thinking about?'

'Kerry,' he said. 'I've a farm there, or rather my father has.'

'And you'd like to go back?'

'It's quite a place. Sea and mountains, green grass, soft rain, fuchsia growing on the dusty hedges, glowing in the evening. *Deorini Dei*—the Tears of God, they call it.' He laughed softly. 'And the prettiest girls in the world. I was almost forgetting.'

He turned and found her looking at him, something that was very close to pain upon her face. Instinctively, he reached out and took her hand. 'You'd fit into the scenery admirably.'

She gazed at him searchingly, the strange, orange light playing upon her face and then her smile seemed to deepen, to become luminous, and he pulled her to her feet and kissed her gently on the parted mouth.

Her lips were soft and fresh and quite suddenly, he was trembling slightly, his stomach hollow with excitement. It was as if she were the first, as if this had never happened before. She turned her face into his coat, holding him tightly and above them, a single cloud of red fire burned itself out, leaving them wordless in the night.

CHAPTER EIGHT

THE morning was cold with no rain, and a trace of mist hung over the fields behind the house as Rogan leaned against the fence, smoking a cigarette, and looked up at Scardale Fell, shrouded by low cloud.

He had spent the night on a camp bed in the old harness room above the barn and had eaten breakfast with Hannah and young Brendan, the others being still abed. Now, feeling relaxed and strangely content, he waited for the girl to bring the car from the barn.

Behind him, the house door opened and Paddy Costello shouted angrily, 'Get out of it, you useless lump. Up on the fellside with you and don't come back without those sheep.'

Young Brendan dodged a kick and ran across the yard, his patched jacket flying behind him. As he passed Rogan, he looked at him quickly, the dark eyes in the thin face like those of some hunted animal and Rogan was aware of an instant sympathy.

The boy ran away along the road and Costello came towards Rogan. His eyes were tinged with yellow, the veins swollen with blood and the pouched and folded skin of his face looked somehow unclean.

'He'll be the death of me, that lad, Mr. Rogan. The death of me.' He pushed the tail of his shirt into his waistband. 'The early start you're getting.'

'I've plenty to do,' Rogan said. 'Are Morgan and Fletcher still in bed?'

The old man nodded. 'What else would you expect from a couple of low-lifes like them two, Mr. Rogan.'

In the barn, an engine coughed into life and the shooting brake emerged, Hannah at the wheel. She stopped and Rogan opened the door and got into the passenger seat beside her. He wound down the window and looked out at her uncle.

'If you're thinking of taking a trip in the cattle truck or the Morris, forget it. I've taken the keys. Tell Morgan I'll be back some time this afternoon.'

As the old man's face slipped, Rogan wound up the window and nodded to Hannah who released the handbrake and took the brake out through the gateway and down the dirt road into the mist.

She was wearing slim-fitting navy-blue ski pants, a heavy sheepskin jacket and a silk scarf was bound around her head, and again, he was conscious of that same restless excitement he had known on the hillside the previous evening.

As if aware that he was watching her she coloured slightly, her eyes never leaving the road as she negotiated a dangerous bend around a shoulder of the mountain.

'Your uncle chased the boy off up the fellside,' he said. 'Something about some sheep.'

She nodded. 'He's been selling them off in half dozen lots lately. He has a powerful thirst. They spend most of their time up there on the slopes. Finding them can be difficult.'

'Shouldn't the boy have a sheepdog?'

'He did. A collie named Thrasher, the joy of his life. He fell into one of the old mine shafts last month and broke his back. Some of them are a couple of hundred feet deep.'

Rogan sat there thinking about it. At breakfast, the boy hadn't had a great deal to say for himself, and when he did speak it was obvious that he stammered badly. Probably only psychological and not surprising with a father like Paddy Costello.

'You don't like my uncle, do you?' she said.

He laughed shortly. 'The understatement of the age. I've met too many of his breed. A big man with the drink taken and words pouring out of him by the hundred. I can see him now in front of a police inspector with a face like whey, the cap twisting in his hands while he spills out his unclean guts. God knows how Colum O'More could have been taken in by him.'

'But he wasn't. My uncle contacted him through an old comrade in Liverpool and Colum simply turned up at the farm a month later. He didn't like what he found. He squeezed my uncle dry with the help of a bottle of pot-distilled whiskey that put him on his back in two hours, then turned his attention to me.'

'Had you ever met before?'

'Never, but he seemed to take to me. He said that he always liked to work from a distance through a go-between. He offered me the job.'

'And you accepted.'

'Remember what you said yesterday about wanting to crash out of something? Well, Colum O'More offered me the chance to do just that. Two thousand pounds and a passage to Ireland with him at the end and he promised to take Brendan with us.'

'And that was important to you?'

She shrugged. 'I couldn't walk out and leave him. Uncle Paddy won't last much longer, not at the rate he's drinking and what would happen to Brendan then? An institution?'

'So you're the only one who knows where Colum's staying? Your uncle wouldn't like that.'

She chuckled. 'He's tried following me a time or two and so has Morgan, but it didn't get them anywhere.'

'You sound as if you've been enjoying yourself?'

'I suppose I have.' She frowned as if trying to explain it to herself and concentrated on the road. 'In a strange way, I've been in a sort of limbo, drifting aimlessly ever since I was released from prison and came to Scardale to live. A year of days passing, the rain falling, snow on the mountains, and somewhere else a world that I had cut myself out of.'

'Surgery is always painful,' he said. 'Some people never get over it.'

She smiled tightly. 'Anyway, like I said yesterday, what else could I have done? There was nowhere else to go. I was in this thing up to my neck whether I liked it or not.'

From Ambleside, they followed the lake to Windermere, then took the road through Staveley to Kendal. There was very little traffic about and the mist, if anything, was a little heavier. In Kendal itself, it was raining heavily and they passed through a thin scattering of traffic and drove out of the town again.

She pointed out the site of the Roman fort of Alavna as solemnly as if he had been any ordinary tourist. 'The Romans never landed in Ireland, did they?'

'They knew better,' Rogan said and a wide grin split across his face.

She glanced at him briefly, a sudden light in her eyes. 'That's the first time you've laughed properly since I've met you. I was beginning to think you didn't know how.'

He smiled again. 'Give me time, Hannah. That's all I need.'

For a brief moment, the intimacy between them was almost physical and they were both aware of the fact. He groped for the right words, but before he could find them, they topped a small rise of the narrow country road and he saw Rigg Station in the hollow below.

She stopped the shooting brake on the edge of a small parking space covered with gravel and Rogan lit a cigarette and wound down the window. The small, single-storeyed building had a roof of red tiles and was constructed of large square blocks of granite. There was an arched entrance, a large clock above it and a scale map of the district was displayed in a glass case pinned to the wall. At the other end was the loading bay, double-doors giving access to the station.

'Let's take a closer look,' Rogan said.

They got out of the brake and crossed the patch of gravel to the entrance. Inside, there was a narrow hall, a barrier and a ticket window which was closed by a wooden shutter. The door to the platform stood open and they could hear cheerful whistling. When Rogan peered cautiously round, he could see an oldish white-haired man sweeping the platform at the far end.

'Keep him talking,' Rogan said to Hannah. 'Ask him if you can still catch the London train from here, anything you like, but keep him on the platform. I'll take a look round.'

She nodded briefly and moved out through the door. The old man didn't see her until she was almost upon him and he leaned on the broom and smiled. As the murmur of their voices started to echo through the quiet station, Rogan moved quickly to the door marked *Stationmaster* and opened it.

Inside he found the usual cluttered office. There was a desk, a couple of wooden filing cabinets and two or three yellowing calendars on the walls. There were two other doors. One gave access to a small washroom, the other to a narrow arched baggage hall which cut through the building from front to rear linking the platform with the loading bay. He moved out on to the concrete bay, jumped to the ground and went back to the car.

When Hannah returned five minutes later, he was smoking a cigarette, hands thrust deep into his pockets, a curiously withdrawn look on his face. She slid behind the wheel and closed the door.

'I thought I was never going to get away. Did you see everything you wanted?'

He nodded. 'What did the old man have to say?'

She smiled. 'His name's Briggs, and he retires next month. He's got two daughters and six grandchildren and his wife died two years ago. He also told me I couldn't get the London train from here, but that was only incidental.'

'He didn't leave much out.'

'I could have been talking to him yet. I don't suppose he has much to do in a place like this. It must get pretty boring. Apparently he isn't here all the time. They just send anyone who's available from Kendal.'

Rogan looked out at the station building again, a slight frown on his face. 'Where were you last Friday when the van arrived?'

'On the other side of the road under that tree,' she said. 'I brought Brendan with me. We had a picnic.'

'Did you get a close look at the driver and the guard when they got out of the van?'

'Close enough.'

'What kind of uniform do they wear?'

'That's easy. I sat next to one of them in a transport café in Kendal last month. A double-breasted blue serge suit with black plastic buttons—the sort of thing Naval Petty Officers wear. The cap was the only elaborate thing about him. Shiny black peak edged with gold and a fancy badge.'

'And the bags the money was in—you saw them, too?'

'As they pulled them out on to the ramp. They were just the usual G.P.O. mailbags. Is it important?'

'It could be.'

He took a large-scale map of the area from the glove compartment and unfolded it across his knees. After a while, he nodded. 'Let's get moving. Take the road back to Kendal then out towards Staveley. About forty miles an hour. No faster. I'll tell you when to stop.'

She drove back into Kendal and took the Windermere road to Staveley. Just before the junction with the Bowness road and perhaps ten minutes after leaving Rigg Station, Rogan nodded and she slowed to a halt. A few yards away, a five-barred gate gave access to a track which disappeared into a plantation of fir trees. Rogan got out of the brake, walked across to the gate and fumbled with the rusty chain that fastened it to an old stone post. The gate swung open and he returned to the car and got in.

'Follow the track and take it easy. According to the map there should be some flooded gravel pits a couple of hundred yards in.'

The track was soggy with rain and overgrown with

grass from long disuse. Hannah stayed in a low gear and took the brake forward cautiously. The fir trees closed in on either side, dark and sombre, and then they went over a small rise and dropped down into a clearing.

There was an old barn constructed of heavy grey stone, its roof gaping to the sky and, beyond it, water gleamed through the undergrowth.

Hannah cut the engine and Rogan got out and walked across. He looked up at the crumbling walls for a moment, then continued across the clearing and paused at the far edge. A mass of undergrowth sprawled in a confusion of twisted branches to spill over the lip of a fifty-foot cliff that lifted from the dark waters of the gravel pit below.

Rogan stood there looking down, the slight frown still on his face. After a while he nodded his head as if in confirmation of some secret, hidden decision, turned and found Hannah standing a couple of yards away watching him.

'Can it be done, Sean Rogan?'

He flicked his cigarette down into the water and smiled calmly. 'I think it's time I had another word with Colum O'More.'

He took her arm, and together they walked back to the brake.

CHAPTER NINE

VANBRUGH cursed as he sank into a patch of bog, cold water slopping over the tops of his rubber boots. The Sergeant and constable of the county constabulary who accompanied him pulled him back on to firm ground with impassive faces and they continued up the slope.

On the crest of the tor, cloud dashed cold rain in the face and mist hung in a damp grey curtain that reduced visibility to no more than fifty yards.

Vanbrugh turned to the Sergeant. 'How long can a man last in conditions like this?'

'You'd be surprised, sir. We've had them on the run for a week many a time. The classic case was the bloke who got out during the winter about five years back. He was on the loose for a fortnight.'

'How did he manage that?'

'Holed up in a holiday cottage no more than three miles from the prison. That's one of the difficulties. There are lots of places like that all over the moor. They're always empty at this time of the year and we can't keep them all under constant surveillance. We haven't got enough men.'

'I know, Sergeant. I know.'

Vanbrugh turned and went back down the hill towards his car and police Land-Rover parked beside it. He was cold and tired and thinking about Sean Rogan somewhere out there in the mist, running like a hunted animal, didn't make him feel any better.

As he neared the two vehicles, another Land-Rover appeared from the mist and pulled in at the side of the road. Sergeant Dwyer got out and moved to meet him.

'Any luck at the other end?' Vanbrugh said.

Dwyer shook his head. 'Not a smell of him so far. The Chief Constable seems to think a house-to-house search should be the next step in case he's holed up somewhere. Apparently there are lots of holiday bungalows and cottages scattered across the moor that are mostly empty out of season.'

'No guarantee he wouldn't pick on one that's already been searched,' Vanbrugh said. 'Did you get that list from the prison?'

Dwyer took a typewritten sheet from his pocket and unfolded it. 'Here you are, sir. They couldn't list his close friends over the past few years because he hasn't had any, but there are at least half a dozen men here who've shared cells with him since he came out of solitary confinement.'

Vanbrugh examined the list quickly. 'Some real villains here. At least one of 'em's back inside to my knowledge.' He frowned and an expression of distaste appeared on his face. 'So he shared a cell with Jack Pope?'

'You know him, sir?'

'I should do. He was a sergeant in the uniformed branch at West End Central. Got sent down for corruption ten or twelve years ago and he's been back inside since for fraud.' Vanbrugh shook his head and said grimly, 'I can't stand a crooked copper.' He handed the list back to Dwyer. 'Anything else?'

'There was a message from the Yard about that lawyer you wanted them to contact, the one who visited Rogan. He doesn't seem to exist.'

Vanbrugh swore softly. 'Then Rogan didn't just take off into the blue. The whole thing was arranged. Why else would a phoney lawyer visit him only a couple of weeks before the event?'

'Which means that Soames must have known that Rogan had a way out, sir, and not many people did. It was kept pretty dark and Rogan doesn't sound the sort of man who'd open his mouth if it didn't suit him.'

'It's amazing what men find out about each other when they share a cell, Sergeant. As far as I'm concerned, any one of those men on that list of yours could have taken the information out with them when they were released.'

The rain suddenly increased in force and they climbed into the rear of the Land-Rover. Vanbrugh took a large vacuum flask from a basket under the seat and poured coffee into two plastic cups.

As he handed one to Dwyer, the Sergeant said, 'If what you surmise is true, sir, Rogan could be almost anywhere by now, perhaps even across to Ireland.'

Vanbrugh shook his head. 'We'd have been the first to know, believe me. He's something of a legend in his own time, remember. His homecoming would hardly pass unnoticed.'

He started to fill his pipe. Dwyer hesitated and then said, 'Do you think we'll get him, sir?'

'I hope not, Sergeant. I hope not.' Vanbrugh looked up with a slight smile, the pipe jutting from the corner of his mouth. 'That surprises you?'

'It mightn't if you explained why, sir.'

'It's really quite simple.' Vanbrugh put a match to his pipe and puffed out blue smoke. 'Sean Rogan's no criminal. He's a political offender. That doesn't mean I think he's right, but it doesn't mean that I have to agree with a system which condemns him to the same treatment as a criminal. In any case, as the I.R.A. has now officially called off its underground campaign, I don't see how any useful purpose can be served by compelling Rogan and men like him to work out their sentences to the bitter end.'

'I must admit it doesn't make sense to me, sir.'

Vanbrugh nodded. 'Which doesn't mean that I'm not going to do my damnedest to run him down and find the men who helped him out.'

'He must be quite a man.'

'And then some.' Vanbrugh flicked the match into the rain and stared into the past. 'I was working on special assignment in France back in '43 and Rogan was running the local underground. Someone opened their mouth and I was picked up by German Military Intelligence.'

'Things must have looked pretty grim.'

'There was a troop train passing through on its way to the Ruhr and they arranged for it to stop at a tiny local station called Blois to pick me up. I was escorted there by two tanks and a company of infantry. They weren't taking any chances on the Maquis interfering.'

'What happened?'

'When we reached Blois, the main escort stayed outside

and I was marched into a small waiting room between two Intelligence officers who'd even taken the precaution of handcuffing themselves to me. Inside, we found Rogan in the uniform of a colonel of infantry and half a dozen of his men. They knocked my escort senseless and released me.'

'Then what?'

'They had an unconscious man on a stretcher, some local collaborator. Rogan took him out on the platform when the train arrived and handed him over in my place and I scrambled into a spare uniform they'd brought me. We then walked out of the waiting room past my escort, climbed into a couple of official cars and drove away. The whole thing couldn't have lasted more than five minutes.'

'By God, it must have taken nerve.'

'And brains. The kind of intelligence that can always find a solution to even the most hopeless situation.' He looked out into the driving rain. 'That's Sean Rogan for you.'

There was a long silence before Dwyer said, 'So you think we might be wasting our time here, sir?'

'We could be,' Vanbrugh said. 'Tell you what you do. Go back to London and see what you can find out about Soames. Try the Law Society for a start. Men who pose as solicitors have usually practised at some time in the past. Have a look through their list of members who've been disbarred during the past few years.'

'And what about the other list, sir?'

'Rogan's old cell-mates?' Vanbrugh nodded. 'Have each one run down and checked. Probably nothing there, but you never can tell at this game.'

'Very well, sir.'

As Dwyer got out of the Land-Rover and walked to his car through the rain, Vanbrugh leaned out and shouted, 'And Dwyer!'

The Sergeant turned. 'Yes, sir?'

'Top priority. We haven't got much time.'

For a moment Dwyer hesitated. It was quite obvious that he intended to say something, but thought better of it and he turned and walked to his car. As he drove away, Vanbrugh leaned back in his seat and took out his matches again, a slight frown on his face.

Now what on earth had made him say that? Time for what? But there was no answer, just that strange sixth sense, product of twenty-five years as a policeman that told him that there was more to all this than any of them realized. Much more.

CHAPTER TEN

RAIN hammered lightly against the window and Colum O'More turned to look outside. 'More rain. It never seems to do anything else.'

He was sitting in his armchair by the fire, his stick beside him and Rogan sat in the opposite chair drinking coffee. He was shocked at the obvious deterioration in the old man's condition. The face was grey, the skin hanging from the great jaw in loose, yellow folds and a two-day growth of beard didn't improve matters.

'When did you last see a doctor?'

O'More shifted uncomfortably in his chair and made an impatient gesture. 'Don't start worrying about me. I look a damned sight worse than I am. We've got something more important to discuss.'

'Suit yourself.' Rogan took out a cigarette and lit it with a splinter of wood from the fire. 'What do you think?'

'Of the plan?' O'More chuckled. 'It has just about the right mixture of simplicity and cold nerve I might have expected from you.'

'You think it could work?'

'I can't see how it could fail, not if you get your timing right.'

'What about flaws?'

The old man stuffed tobacco into his pipe, a slight frown on his face. 'There's a goods train due in at Rigg half an hour after the mail train. Unloads things like cattle fodder and heavy machinery for local farmers.'

Rogan shrugged. 'That would still give us a margin of twenty-five minutes to get away.'

'But you couldn't get across here in that time and once the news is out, the whole area will be buzzing with peelers. There aren't many roads through these mountains, remember. They'll have no trouble in closing them.'

'As long as we can make it back to Costello's farm at Scardale I'll be satisfied. We'll come here on Saturday.'

O'More frowned. 'They'll be stopping everything in sight.'

'I've got an idea that should take care of that.' Hannah came in from the kitchen with fresh coffee and he held out his cup. 'The worst thing you can do in that sort of situation is to get hold of a fast car. I proved that time and time again in the old days with the Resistance in France. A battered old van or truck that had all on to do twenty miles an hour with a load of hay or turnips or a couple of pigs in the back was the best bet. The important thing is to look as if you belong, as if you're just going about your normal business.'

'Which is logical enough. What have you in mind?'

Rogan turned to Hannah. 'You said your uncle had been selling off his sheep lately? Where exactly?'

'Sometimes to some wholesale butchers in Kendal, sometimes at cattle auctions on market days.'

'Is there a market anywhere on this side on a Saturday?'

She nodded. 'Millom. That's about five or six miles south of here.'

'Good enough,' Rogan said. 'We'll drive over in Paddy Costello's old cattle truck with a dozen or fifteen sheep in the back. I don't think the police will give us much trouble.'

'There'll be plenty of other farmers on the same road,' Hannah said.

'That's settled then.'

Colum O'More nodded, a slight frown on his face. 'There's just one thing I'm not happy about. From what I know of the way this security van firm works generally, the driver will contact County Police Headquarters on the radio telephone twice. Once to signal his arrival at Rigg, and then again to let them know that the job's complete. How are you going to get over that second call? If the police don't get it, they'll send out a local car to check straight away, just as a matter of routine.'

'I thought of that one, too,' Rogan said. 'There's only one way out. We'll have to get them to phone in for us from the mail train. Tell them the set's gone dead in the van or there's been an accident or something. It's reasonable enough. That sort of thing must happen occasionally.'

They sat there in silence for several moments and then the old man slapped his knee. 'By God, I think it'll go, Sean.' He turned to the girl. 'What do you say, Hannah?'

'You're the experts.' She picked up the tray. 'I'll make something to eat.'

She returned to the kitchen and O'More laughed.

'You've taken ten years off me already.'

'Don't speak too soon.' Rogan walked to the window and looked out at the rain. 'Soames and Jack Pope, how much are they mixed up in this thing?'

'They aren't,' Colum said. 'They were paid in advance for their part. As far as I'm concerned, they don't even know where we are or what we're doing. I've seen Soames in person once. Pope I only know from a photograph. Since then I've used the Kendal accommodation address in the name of Charles Grant. I've covered my tracks

81

every step of the way. That's why I decided to use Hannah as a go-between. Even her uncle doesn't know about this place.'

'I didn't like the way Pope was playing things. The night I crashed out, after I left, I parked the car down the road and went back on foot. He and Soames had their heads together in the living room of the cottage.'

The old man frowned. 'So what?'

'Jack Pope's in Ambleside now. He's already been in contact with Morgan. Hannah overheard him and Fletcher talking about it. From what she said, her uncle's in it up to the tide mark on his dirty neck.'

'The lousy bastards,' the old man said. 'They've sold me out.'

'You let Soames recruit them for you. The link was there from the start. How much have Morgan and Fletcher had already?'

'Five hundred each. The rest to be paid out two weeks after the job's finished, through a man I know in Liverpool.'

Rogan shook his head. 'Not enough, Colum. These men are professionals. When they work for wages they expect half in advance, half after the job's finished. You should have smelt a rat the minute they said they were willing to accept such a small advance.'

'And how would I be knowing that?' Colum O'More demanded angrily. 'When have I needed to work with riffraff like this before?'

'No cause for alarm.' Rogan held up a hand and smiled coldly. 'This thing is beginning to interest me.'

'And me, too, by God.'

The old man leaned across to the table, opened a drawer and produced a heavy Colt automatic of the type used by American officers during the war. He tossed it across.

Rogan caught it deftly, extracted the magazine, checked it, then rammed it back into the butt. 'A long time since I handled one of these.'

'I'm not suggesting you leave any corpses around when you've finished, but it might come in handy,' the old man said. 'When do you think they'll make their move?'

'At the farm after the job's finished. If they tried anything earlier, they might really mess things up. I don't think Morgan's that stupid.'

Colum cursed and slammed his hand hard against his bad leg. 'I have to sit here, crippled and useless and you alone.'

'There's always Hannah. At least I can rely on her.' Rogan got to his feet. 'Don't worry, Colum, there's always a certain strength in knowing the opposition for what it is.'

Hannah came in from the kitchen, belting her raincoat. 'Are you ready?'

'As ever was.' Rogan punched the old man heavily on the shoulder. 'Every tinker to his own trade, Colum, and this is mine. The one thing I had a talent for.'

He went outside. It was raining heavily and he ran across the yard, scrambled into the shooting brake and switched on the radio. It was almost half past the hour and a few moments later, the news headlines came on. As he was listening, Hannah opened the other door and got behind the wheel.

There was a political crisis in the Far East, car workers were on strike again and the Opposition seriously disagreed with the Government's policy towards immigration. The final item was a brief mention of the fact that Rogan was still at large, that the moor was being combed thoroughly and that the Chief Constable confidently expected his early recapture.

Rogan switched off and turned with a slight smile. 'So far, so good. Let's get back to the farm.'

She moved into gear and took the brake back along the rutted track towards the main road.

CHAPTER ELEVEN

'I'LL go over it again,' Rogan said.

He leaned across the table, the map spread before him and they crowded around, Fletcher almost knocking over the oil lamp in his eagerness.

'Paddy leaves here first in the cattle truck and parks it at the gravel pits this side of Kendal. We follow five minutes later in the Morris van, Hannah at the wheel, the rest of us in the back with the dummy sacks. We pick Paddy up on the way.' He glanced at Morgan. 'You and Fletcher will be in uniform as I've described.'

'The post of honour,' Morgan said mockingly.

'There isn't one. We get to Rigg no more than five minutes before the armoured van. I go in with Paddy, handle the stationmaster. Hannah backs up to the loading bay and you two get those sacks inside on the double. Then Hannah takes off and waits at the gravel pits.'

Hannah nodded calmly and Rogan went on, 'Paddy gets into the stationmaster's uniform and starts to sweep the platform. We wait for the armoured van.'

'They don't get out till he tells them the train's coming,' Morgan said. 'That doesn't leave much time.'

'We'll have to work fast, that's all. The moment they drag the first couple of sacks off the loading bay into the baggage hall, you smack them down good and hard. We aren't playing patty fingers.'

'Then what?'

'You and Fletcher put on their caps. That's the one part of the uniform we can't duplicate.'

'What if they don't fit?'

'Make them fit. Wear them at an angle—anything. Then open the door and out with the dummy sacks.'

'How many?'

'God knows. We'll take six. If there's more, they'll have to have some money back. That kind of a sack stuffed with notes can weigh as much as a hundredweight. We don't have time to mess about.'

'What happens on the platform?'

'You play it by ear. According to Colum, the duty men on the train change as often as the van crews so nobody should question you. There'll be a clearance chit. Get it signed, crack a joke and that's it.'

'What about the stationmaster? How do we know they'll accept Paddy in his place?'

'No trouble there. They don't have a regular stationmaster at Rigg. They send out anyone available from Kendal.'

There was a small silence and Fletcher glanced at Morgan. 'What do you think?'

'Looks good to me.' He turned to Rogan. 'What about mailbags? They're not easy to come by, not in a place like this.'

'I was hoping you might be able to suggest something.'

'I know a bloke in Manchester who's good at that sort of thing.'

'Fine,' Rogan said. 'You and Fletcher can take a run down in the brake in the morning. You could pick yourself up a couple of uniforms at one of those war surplus places.'

'Suits me,' Morgan said. 'I could do with a look at the big city again.'

'No hanging around,' Rogan said. 'I want you back here by dark, and lay off that stuff,' he told Fletcher, who was pouring whisky into a tumbler at the sideboard. 'You'll need all your wits about you on Friday.'

'You mind your business, Jack, I'll mind mine,' Fletcher said and moved out into the passage.

Morgan lit a cigarette and flicked the match into the fire. 'Just one thing bothers me—what happens when we get back here?'

'We sit tight till Saturday, then go our separate ways.'

'When do we slice up the cake?'

'We don't. You get what's coming to you from O'More's agent in Liverpool a fortnight later as agreed.'

'Why not here on the great day?'

'You disappoint me, Morgan. I thought you had brains.' Rogan shook his head. 'We'll stick to the contract.'

'All right for you,' Morgan said. 'You've got your line of retreat worked out, but what about Fletcher and me? There'll be more scuffers than hikers on these roads before you know where you are.'

'Then lie up here for a week or two. Move out when the fuss dies down.'

Morgan nodded. 'Maybe you've got something there.' He yawned. 'Think I'll take a walk before turning in.'

'You do that.'

When he had gone, Paddy Costello laughed nervously and clapped his hands together. 'God save us, but it's the great day, Mr. Rogan, and me feeling like a young 'un again. I'll just take a wee walk along to the kitchen and see what damage Fletcher's done to that bottle of mine.'

He went out and Hannah got up from the chair where she had sat in silence throughout the whole proceedings. 'What about Morgan? Do you think he's gone to phone Pope?'

'That's what I intend to find out. You hold the fort here. I won't be long.'

He hurried along the passage, took down a three-quarter length oilskin coat from a peg and opened the door. Rain drummed down against the roof, bouncing from the cobbles, silver in the broad band of yellow light that streamed from the window of the living room. She stood in the window watching him, curiously still, her face grave and, for some unaccountable reason, a great tenderness moved inside him so that he wanted to reach out, to touch her face gently, tell her that he cared. But there was no time, probably never would be.

He hurried along the track in the darkness, keeping to

the grass shoulder, for half a mile until he reached the main road. He saw Morgan at once, standing in the lighted telephone box a hundred yards down the road. Rogan moved towards the box, keeping in the shadows, and paused in the shelter of the bush no more than ten yards away.

Morgan was speaking into the receiver and, after a while, he put it down. He opened the door, looked out at the heavy rain and lit a cigarette.

Rogan waited, rain soaking his head, streaming across his face. Once a truck passed going down towards Ambleside, but otherwise, Morgan in the lighted telephone box might have been the only inhabitant of a dark world.

It was perhaps twenty minutes after Morgan had made his telephone call that Rogan heard the sound of an engine faintly through the rain from the direction of Ambleside. A moment later, a mini-car braked to a halt and Jack Pope leaned out of the window.

Morgan got in beside him and they started to talk. It was impossible for Rogan to hear anything of their conversation at all. He watched for a moment or two more, then withdrew into the darkness and started back along the road to the farm.

Whatever it was they intended, they meant business, so much was certain. But where was Soames and what was he doing? That was the important thing. Or perhaps he was simply the man behind the scenes? God knows, he'd hardly looked like the active type.

The rain seemed to increase in force and Rogan bent his head and pushed on. As he rounded the shoulder of the hill, the valley falling away steeply on his right, he could see the farm nestling in a hollow of darkness, the yellow light reaching out into the night, and Hannah screamed his name aloud.

He was running, splashing in puddles of water and not caring, a strange sense of unreality to everything and saw her, silhouetted in the doorway, her hands clawing at Fletcher's face as he towered above her.

Brendan was on his knees in a pool of water, dazed and shaken, blood on his face, and Rogan ran forward lightly, a terrible, cold anger surging through him. The girl's dress was torn to the waist and as Fletcher laughed drunkenly and bent to kiss her, she jerked her head away so that Rogan got a clear picture of her face. There was nothing of fear there, only rage and humiliation and disgust. He grabbed Fletcher by the collar and pulled him away in one easy movement.

Fletcher staggered backwards, lost his balance and fell to one knee. He stayed there for a moment, looking up at Rogan, an expression of bewilderment on his brutal face, then gave a cry of anger and flung himself forward, hands reaching out to rend flesh and muscle.

Rogan swayed to one side and slashed him across the kidneys with the edge of his hand as the big man ran headlong past. Fletcher screamed and hit the wall. As he turned, Rogan punched him with tremendous force beneath the breastbone, the sound of the blow like a mallet striking wood. Fletcher slid down on his knees, the breath coming out of him in a long sigh.

Rogan moved in close and incredibly, one gnarled hand grabbed for his ankle and pulled hard, jerking him off balance so that he fell heavily to the cobbles. Fletcher's great hand clawed across his body, reaching for the throat. Rogan grabbed at his wrists and they rolled over in the rain.

They cannoned into the wall beside the horse trough and Rogan, with a supreme effort, threw him to one side and got to his feet. Fletcher reached for the edge of the trough and pulled himself up. As he reached his full height, Rogan moved in fast and kicked him in the stomach. Fletcher doubled over and a knee like iron lifted into his face sending him back over the edge of the water trough.

He sprawled there, head under the surface and Rogan leaned on the edge to get his breath. After a while, he grabbed the big man by the shirt front and hauled him

88

out. He dropped him on the cobbles and turned to find Hannah and Morgan watching him.

When he spoke, his voice seemed to be the voice of a stranger and the blood pounded in his ears. 'You tell him next time I see him with a bottle, I'll break it over his skull.' He pushed Morgan violently out of the way and lurched across the yard towards the house.

He was sitting in the chair beside the kitchen table, he was aware of that, and Hannah was wiping the blood from his face with a towel and warm water, tears pouring down her cheeks, and then she was in his arms and his lips were against the cool flesh and it was as if this had always been.

Outside in the rain, Morgan crouched beside Fletcher who was moaning in pain, eyes half open. 'What was it you called him, Jesse? Just a big Irish bogtrotter? Hit him in the right place and he'd split clean down the middle.'

He started to laugh, turned and walked to the house and left Fletcher lying there alone in the heavy rain.

CHAPTER TWELVE

MORGAN and Fletcher left for Manchester straight after breakfast the following morning, Fletcher sullen and angry, his eyes smouldering with hate whenever he looked at Rogan.

Rogan stood at the gate and watched the brake move away down the dirt road. He turned and looked up at the mountains, feeling relaxed and at peace. The morning was bright and clean, the moor purple with heather and the haze of autumn was on the land.

He turned and found Hannah watching him, a slight smile on her face. 'A fine morning.'

'With those two gone it's like being rid of a bad taste in your mouth.' He took a deep breath as a small wind lifted from the stream in the valley bringing with it the dank, wet smell of rotting leaves.

'My favourite season, autumn,' Hannah said. 'Always something a little sad about it. Old dreams like smoke in the air, lingering on for a moment before fading for ever.'

There was a poignancy in her voice that touched something deep inside him and he reached out and caressed her face gently with the back of his hand. She turned and kissed his palm, her face flushed and beautiful.

'What would you like to do?' he said. 'The way I see it, we've got the day to ourselves.'

She turned, shading her eyes, and looked up at the fells. 'I'd like to go up there, I think. It would be nice to be above the world for an hour or two. I could make some sandwiches.'

'Sounds fine to me,' Rogan said. 'What about your uncle?'

'Still sleeping it off. Brendan went up the valley half an hour ago. We'll probably see him up there.'

They returned to the house. Hannah went into the kitchen and Rogan had a shave. When he had finished, he helped himself to the oilskin jacket he had used the night before and an old tweed cap from a peg behind the door, and waited outside.

Hannah joined him a few minutes later. She was wearing leather knee-length boots and jeans and her sheepskin jacket. A scarf was knotted around her head and she carried an old army knapsack.

'I'll take that,' Rogan said and he slipped his arms through the straps.

Over the mountains, the sky was grey and threatening and the sun had almost disappeared, but the prospect of more rain didn't seem to matter. They turned out through the gate and started up the valley.

The surface of the old road had almost disappeared under a creeping carpet of moss and rank grass that grew profusely from every crack and it followed the side of the hill, rising steeply. Beyond a shoulder they paused and saw in a hollow beneath them the ruins of the old mining village.

As they moved down, rain descended in a great rush, splashing into the interiors of the roofless cottages, giving the place a setting that was somehow strangely appropriate.

'It must have been quite a place,' Rogan said.

Hannah nodded. 'I looked it up in the library in Ambleside once. There were two or three hundred people living here at one time. They mined for lead during the Napoleonic Wars.'

'What happened?'

'The vein ran out during the eighteen twenties.' She sighed. 'It's rather sad when you come to think of it. This place was once alive and throbbing with love and laughter and children and chapel on Sundays and then the vein ran out.'

'That's life,' Rogan said gently. 'The vein always seems to run out when you least expect it.'

She turned, a shadow in her eyes. 'It isn't really fair, is it? It doesn't seem to give people much. You work and hope and then get kicked in the teeth.'

'God lets no man suffer too long.' Rogan smiled. 'A saying my grandmother was fond of.'

'Do you believe that?'

He shrugged. 'I believe in hope, Hannah. Hope above all things. Without it, life would be pretty pointless.'

They paused outside the little church and Rogan examined the slab above the door with the faded letters, moss-grown: *Scardale Primitive Methodist Chapel* 1805.

'The year of Trafalgar,' he said. 'A long time ago.'

'Another British victory?'

He grinned. 'There were more than fifty American

91

citizens in the crew of Nelson's *Victory* and twice as many Irishmen. A way the British had with them.'

'We learn something new every day.'

They moved on, following the slope of the main street and came to a sizeable dam constructed of large blocks of granite stone, slippery and green with the years where moisture leaked through, the stream issuing from a stone sluice at the bottom.

On the far side of the dam higher up the valley were the actual mine workings. A dozen or fifteen sheep were penned together in an old stone enclosure. A few yards away, Brendan Costello sat on a large boulder throwing pebbles into the water. Hannah called to him and he turned quickly, eyes very dark in the white face.

He came towards them and nodded to Rogan, smiling shyly. Hannah ruffled his hair with obvious affection. 'What have you been doing?'

He spoke in short, rather clipped sentences, an obvious attempt to defeat his stammer by missing out those words which gave him most difficulty.

'He w-wants m-more sheep bringing down.'

Hannah nodded. 'We're having our dinner up here today. Would you like to come with us?'

He looked swiftly at Rogan and his face crimsoned with pleasure. 'C-can I?'

'If you like.'

'I c-could show you the Long C-cut, Mr. Rogan. Y-you'd like that.'

Rogan turned to Hannah. 'The Long Cut?'

She pointed to the western end of the dam where it ran into a tangled mass of bushes at the face of a steep cliff. 'We'll take a look if you like. You can't see the entrance from here, but they ran a tunnel under the shoulder of the mountain into the next valley. It carries a canal. They used to take the ore out that way.'

They moved round the edge of the dam into a clump of trees, and beyond them a crumbling landing stage jutted into the water and the mouth of the tunnel gaped darkly. There was very little headroom and when Rogan squatted down and looked inside, he could see a tiny circle of light at the other end.

'How long is it?'

'Six or seven hundred yards.'

He whistled softly. 'It must have taken some doing.'

'There was a natural cave system. I think they just linked it up. Of course there wouldn't be any water in it until they built the dam.'

'Quite an achievement all the same.'

'We can go through if you like.'

She pointed, and when Rogan turned he saw the boy moving out of the undergrowth at the side of the dam hauling on a length of rope, to which was attached a heavy, high-sided punt of the type used by wildfowlers. There was a couple of inches of water in the bottom.

Rogan grinned. 'Are you sure it's safe?'

Hannah dropped into it and sat on one of the narrow wooden seats. 'You couldn't get any wetter than you are.'

Rogan joined her in a world of cold, clammy darkness, of walls that oozed moisture where water constantly dripped so low that Rogan actually had to bend his head, and when he looked over his shoulder he saw that the boy was lying on his back and propelling the punt along by walking his feet along the roof.

They passed into a large echoing cavern with a vaulted roof, crossed it and entered the tunnel again. They passed through two similar caves and then moved into the final stretch, and the opening at the other end seemed to increase in size quite suddenly.

They drifted out into another similar dam and bumped against the side of a stone landing stage. Brendan scrambled up and fastened the line to a rusting iron ring. Rogan followed him and turned to give Hannah a hand up.

They walked through a grove of trees past several ruined buildings. One of them, a stable, had a corrugated

93

iron roof, and stout wooden doors of recent origin were secured with a padlock and chain.

'What's in here?' Rogan asked.

Brendan ran forward, slipped his hand under a flat stone beside the door and produced a key. He quickly unlocked the padlock, pulled away the chain and swung back the door.

An old jeep was parked inside. It had been fitted with a battered aluminium body in place of the old canvas tilt and the original olive green paintwork was chipped and scraped.

Rogan took off his knapsack and got behind the wheel. 'A long time since I drove one of these. It must be all of twenty years old.' He pulled out the choke and pressed the starter and the engine turned over at once. 'Who owns it?'

'Most of this valley is one big sheep ranch run by a syndicate,' Hannah said. 'That's the way farming seems to be going these days. They always keep a jeep or a Land-Rover up here fuelled and ready for action. They're particularly good in bad weather on the fellside. The shepherds use them as they used to use a horse or a pony in the old days.'

Rogan got out of the jeep and they moved back outside. Brendan locked the door and replaced the key under the stone. Below them in the rain, the valley dropped down towards a shining expanse of water.

'What's that?' Rogan said.

'Rydal Water. If you move down the slope a little further you'll see the beginning of Grasmere to the west of it.'

He took an Ordnance Survey Map of the area from the pocket of his jacket and opened it, dropping to one knee. 'Let's suppose something had gone wrong with my original plan and I wanted to get from here to Marsh-End, how would I set about it?'

She examined the map with a slight frown. 'There *is* a back road. I found it by accident one day when Uncle

Paddy tried to follow me. I think I can show you if we move further down the slope.'

They went down the track for perhaps a hundred yards. From that point, it was possible to see not only Rydal Water, but most of Grasmere as well.

'Can you see the stream linking the two lakes?' Hannah asked. 'There's a gate and a small bridge and beyond it a track goes as far as Elterwater. From there, there's a road, mainly unfenced, that takes you through Wrynose Pass between the mountains. About six miles from there, the road branches. If you take the one which follows the valley of the Duddon River through Seathwaite and Ulpha, you come to the Whicham road about ten miles further on.'

'And how far is Whicham from there?'

'Nine or ten miles.'

'And Marsh-End is only a couple of miles from there up the coast.' He nodded and folded the map. 'A lonely sort of road, would you say?'

'You probably wouldn't see a soul during the entire run. Not at this time of the year. Mind you, it could be hard going in bad weather over Wrynose. You'd need a good vehicle, especially if you had a load on. Uncle Paddy's old cattle truck would never make it.'

'I wouldn't be using it, not in the sort of situation I've been going over in my mind.' He lit a cigarette and put one foot on a boulder, resting an elbow on his knee. 'Scardale would be one hell of a place to be caught in with that one road out. It seems to me that in an emergency Brendan's Long Cut would provide a very adequate back door and that jeep would be more than handy.'

'Are you thinking of dropping the idea of using the cattle truck?'

He shook his head. 'Not unless I have to. Does your uncle know about the Long Cut?'

She nodded. 'He's never been through, though. As far as I know, he doesn't think it's possible.'

'So Morgan and Fletcher don't know about it either?'
Rogan nodded, a slight smile on his face. 'We'll keep it
that way. What happens now?'

Hannah looked up through the rain at the top of
Scardale Fell, low cloud and mist draped across it. 'We
could climb up to the top. There's a climbers' hut we
could eat in. Brendan could take the boat back through
the tunnel and climb up the other side to meet us.'

The boy nodded eagerly, turned and ran back through
the trees towards the old landing stage, and Rogan and
the girl took a winding track that slanted up the side of
the fell between rain-soaked, decaying bracken.

After a while, the track narrowed and Hannah went in
front to lead the way. Rogan watched her as she bent to
the slope of the hill, and when she paused and smiled
back at him over her shoulder realized with a sense of
wonder that she was beautiful.

'How are you doing?'

'Never mind about me,' he said. 'We've a thousand feet
or more to go yet.'

He plodded on through the heavy rain and as the
mountain lifted before him he was filled with a strange
feeling that all this had happened before. What was it
the psychologists called it—*déjà vu*? Previously seen?
And then in one quick moment of complete recall he
remembered.

September 1943. Out of France through the Pyrenees
into Spain with papers that had to be in Gibraltar within
a week. It had rained like hell and to make matters
worse, a company of German mountain troops had got
their scent.

He remembered how it had been on just such a hillside
as this, his guide, a brown-skinned Basque mountaineer,
a couple of yards in front. And then the rifle shot, flat,
curiously muffled by the rain. The man had spun round,
a dark hole between his eyes, surprise on his face and
Rogan had jumped into the bracken and run for his
life.

He came back to the present with a start, realizing that Hannah was calling to him. When he looked up, she was standing beside a low hut constructed of great slabs of stone and concrete about fifty feet above him on the edge of a small plateau.

'Any sign of Brendan?' he said as he joined her.

She shook her head. 'It'll take him another twenty minutes at least. Harder going on that side of the mountain.'

Inside the hut there were wooden benches, a table and kindling for a fire. They sat at the table and Rogan took off the knapsack. Hannah produced several packets of sandwiches, some fruit and a large vacuum flask. 'Shall we start or do you want to wait for Brendan?'

'We'll have a coffee and wait.'

He lit a cigarette and they sat there in companionable silence. After a while, she said hesitatingly, 'Is it going to work, Sean?'

He nodded and there was a calm certainty in his voice. 'It'll work all right.'

'And then what?'

'I'll go home,' he said. 'Back to Kerry and that farm I was telling you about.'

'And a good woman?'

He touched her gently on the face. 'I'm twenty years too old for you, have you considered that?'

'You've been in prison a long time,' she said, and a small devil looked out of her eye at him. 'Working that off should keep me going for quite a time.'

Laughter erupted from his throat and he reached across, tugging at her hair. 'The most dangerous remark you ever made in your life, my girl.'

She held on to his hand, her laughter matching his, and then it faded and she turned her face and kissed his palm. He went round the table in two quick steps, the bench going over with a clatter and pulled her into his arms. There were tears on her face and her whole body was trembling. He held her at arm's length and raised her chin with one hand.

'This is one hell of a place to be putting a question like this to you, but did anyone ever ask you to marry him before?'

He could not have stilled her more completely with a slap across the face. She stared at him in incredulous wonder, eyes wide and staring and then she stumbled into his arms, her head against his chest.

When she looked up, her eyes were shining. 'Nothing matters now. Nothing.'

'I know, Hannah. I know.'

There was the rattle of stones on the hillside above the little plateau, she pulled away from him quickly and wiped her eyes. She turned to the table and started to unpack the sandwiches as Brendan appeared in the doorway.

He came forward shyly and Rogan patted him on the shoulder. 'Sit down, son, we've been waiting for you.'

Brendan took the sandwich Hannah offered him, bit into it and sighed with pleasure. The strange thing was that when he spoke there was no trace of a stammer at all. 'I wish this day could go on for ever, Mr. Rogan. Do you ever feel like that?'

Rogan looked across at Hannah, knowing what she must be thinking and shook his head. 'Nothing lasts for ever, son, that's one of the things we all have to learn.'

Hannah's eyes clouded for a moment, her face became a blank mask again. Rogan sighed, got to his feet and moved to the door. The rain was falling harder than ever and he looked out at it morosely. Whichever way you looked at it, life was neither a beginning nor an ending, but a constant state that covered every action a man had taken, good or bad, during his entire existence.

He was involved with this girl just as he was involved with Colum O'More and Harry Morgan, because every single thing he had done in his life had led him to this point. There was no point in regretting anything. Subtract any part of the whole and it no longer existed, which was an interesting thought. He sighed heavily and went back inside.

In the late afternoon as the shadows drifted in across the mountains they moved down the track towards the farm. As they rounded the shoulder of the hill, the shooting brake was turning through the gate into the yard. The two men got out, Fletcher went straight inside, but Morgan stood waiting for them.

'A hell of a day for a walk on the mountain,' he said, the characteristic sardonic smile tugging at the corner of his mouth.

'Any trouble?' Rogan said.

Morgan shook his head. He moved to the rear of the brake, opened the door and lifted a rug to disclose four mailbags neatly folded and a couple of brown paper parcels containing the uniforms.

'Four was all you could get?'

Morgan nodded. 'He had these in stock, so to speak. He could have got us more this evening, but I decided you wouldn't want us to hang around.'

Hannah and Brendan had gone into the house and the two men stood there alone in the heavy rain. 'That's it then,' Rogan said. 'All we can do now is wait.'

'That's all,' Morgan said and there was a slight, mocking edge to his voice.

Rogan looked at him steadily for a long moment. Only when Morgan flushed and looked away did he turn and walk to the house.

CHAPTER THIRTEEN

IT was just before noon on Thursday when Vanbrugh arrived at Paddington. Dwyer was waiting for him at the ticket barrier. They went into the station restaurant, ordered coffee and sat in a corner.

Vanbrugh looked tired and lit a cigarette, an unusual thing for him. 'Any sign of Pope yet?'

'I've managed to trace him to another address, since I wired you the photos of him and those other two prospects yesterday. Not far from here as a matter of fact. His landlady says he moved out a week ago with no forwarding address. I've got some men on it, but it's pretty difficult. You know what the manpower position is in the C.I.D. at the moment.'

'You don't need to tell me.' Vanbrugh ran a hand over his face. 'As it happens, you can stop looking. Pope's been out of town.'

'You've found him, sir?'

Vanbrugh shook his head. 'All I can tell you is that he hired a car in Taunton last weekend. The manager of the place recognized him at once from the photo you sent.'

'Hiring a car's hardly a criminal offence, sir.'

'Perhaps, but being in the area of the prison when his old cell-mate breaks out very probably is.'

'So you think Rogan's no longer in the vicinity of the prison?'

Vanbrugh chuckled. 'What is it they say? No one ever gets off the moor? Well Rogan did and very probably within an hour of getting over the wall, from the way things are beginning to shape up.'

'Then he *must* be in Ireland by now, sir. This is the fourth day, remember.'

Vanbrugh shook his head. 'If he'd landed in Ireland, we'd have known about it, take my word for that. No, he's still in England, I'm certain of that. But why, that's the question.'

He stared down into his cup, a slight frown on his face. 'What about Soames?'

'I've got Scott on the final trace now. I think it's the right man. Real name Bertram Greaves. He was disbarred by the Law Society for malpractice ten years ago. Since then he's been mixed up in all sorts of things under various aliases. Soames must only be the latest of a dozen or more.'

'Any form?'

'Six months for false pretences in 1958. That was unusual. He's the sort who usually manage to skate on pretty thin ice without falling in.'

'Let's hope Scott comes up with something then. In the meantime, I'd like to see Pope's landlady. We're probably wasting our time, but you never can tell.'

Dwyer had a squad car waiting and they pulled up outside a narrow brownstone house in a mean street within ten minutes of leaving the station. The woman who opened the door to them was cold and hard, a cigarette dangling from one corner of her narrow mouth. Beneath the cheap silk scarf, her head was a mass of tightly rolled curlers.

'For Christ's sake, you again?' she said pleasantly when she saw Dwyer.

'Less of that,' he told her. 'Chief Superintendent Vanbrugh would like a word with you.'

Something close to respect appeared on her face and she opened the door wide. 'You'd better come inside.'

There was a stale smell compounded of urine and cooking odours, and an unwashed child, naked from the waist down, stood by the kitchen door and looked at them with wide eyes, a grimy finger in its mouth.

The woman took them up the stairs and opened a door at one side. 'He lived here for a week. I've got a Jamaican moving in Monday. A bloody sight cleaner than some of the bastards we get,' she added defensively.

The room was quite bare except for an old-fashioned wardrobe, a brass bedstead and a strip of linoleum. They went back downstairs and she led the way into the cluttered kitchen.

She stood with her back to the fire, one hand on the mantelpiece. 'I told your man here all I knew, Mr. Vanbrugh. I wish I knew where he was, honest I do. He owed me for his week's rent.'

'There's nothing you can remember? Nothing at all?' Vanbrugh said. 'A word, a name, anything?'

She shook her head stubbornly. 'Nothing.'

'No visitors, even?'

'If you mean birds, I don't run that sort of place.'

Vanbrugh sighed. 'What you're saying is that during the time he lived here, Jack Pope didn't have any kind of contact with anyone. Not even a letter.'

'That's right.' She nodded vigorously and Vanbrugh turned towards the door. 'Of course he did get a postcard one day. Last week I think it was.'

Vanbrugh's tiredness vanished at once. 'A postcard? Where from?'

'For Christ's sake, Mr. Vanbrugh, how would I know?'

'Was it from a seaside place?' Dwyer suggested.

She shook her head. 'No, nowhere like that. I remember being a bit surprised.' Her face brightened. 'Windermere—that was it. Lake Windermere.'

Dwyer looked blankly at Vanbrugh. 'She must be joking, sir. Who in creation would Pope know in the Lake District?'

Vanbrugh turned to the landlady. 'You've been very helpful. Perhaps more than you realize.'

She shrugged. 'I know which side my bread's buttered on, Mr. Vanbrugh. If you do see that sod, you tell him I want my rent.'

The child started to cry and as she moved towards it with a curse, Vanbrugh and Dwyer left hurriedly. As they went down the steps towards the car, the driver leaned out of the window. 'H.Q. on the radio, sir. They've got a message for you. Top priority.'

Vanbrugh nodded to Dwyer. 'You take it. Let's hope it's something good.'

Dwyer leaned in the window and Vanbrugh lit another cigarette, a slight frown knitting his brow. The Lake District. Now that *was* a turn-up for the book. Hardly the sort of place one would expect to hear about from a man like Pope or the sort of people he associated with.

Dwyer turned, excitement on his face. 'That was Scott, sir. He's traced Soames to an address in Hendon. He told the landlady he was going away for a week on business. That was last Saturday. She hasn't seen him since.'

'Let's get moving,' Vanbrugh said. 'This is beginning to get interesting.'

They moved into a calmer, more ordered, world of respectable semi-detached houses with neat hedges and, in spite of the season, well-kept gardens. There was little doubt that whatever else Soames and Pope had in common, it certainly wasn't a similar standard of living.

They found Scott waiting in his car outside a small detached house at one end of a quiet cul-de-sac. He was a tall, quiet young man with a clipped moustache that gave him rather a military air.

'Anything doing?' Vanbrugh demanded.

Scott shook his head. 'He moved out last Saturday. Told her he'd be away for a week on business. She hasn't heard of him since.'

Vanbrugh nodded. 'You stay here. We'll go in. What's her name?'

'Mrs. Jones, sir. A widow lady and very upset about this, I might add.'

She had opened the door as soon as they had ascended the steps, a sure sign that she had been watching from behind the curtains. She was a rather fussy, pouchy-faced woman, with pale blue eyes and wearing a green dress.

'Mrs. Jones? I'm Chief Superintendent Vanbrugh and

this is Detective Sergeant Dwyer. I'd like to ask you a few questions about a man called Soames. I believe he's been staying here.'

'Really, Superintendent, I told the young man who called here earlier everything I know.'

'There may have been a point or two he missed,' Vanbrugh said patiently. 'Perhaps we could see Mr. Soames' room?'

She led the way upstairs, talking incessantly. 'What my other guests are going to think of all this I really don't know and Mr. Soames seemed a most respectable gentleman. A solicitor, he told me. Somewhere in the City.'

'How long has he been staying here?'

'Since early May of this year. Just six months.'

She opened the door at the end of a lengthy passage and led the way in. The room was neat and comfortable. There was a modern washbasin in one corner, two fitted wardrobes and a neat single bed. At the other end, beyond a room divider crammed with books, was a fireplace, a desk, a couple of easy chairs and a french window leading on to a small balcony which overlooked the garden.

'Scott told me he'd been through everything, sir,' Dwyer said. 'Couldn't find anything in writing at all.'

Vanbrugh moved to the desk and opened the drawers one after another in quick succession. They were all quite empty. 'A cautious bird, our Mr. Soames,' he commented.

Dwyer went through the two wardrobes quickly and draped various items across the bed. There was a dressing gown, two suits and several shirts on hangers. Vanbrugh joined him and they went through the pockets.

There were one or two old bus tickets and the odd coin, but nothing else of value, and the drawers of the dressing table contained only underwear, socks and towels.

Mrs. Jones had been watching them with a mixture of uncertainty and horror on her face. At any moment,

Vanbrugh expected her to ask to see the search warrant he didn't have and he moved in to the attack without any further waste of time.

'You told Constable Scott that Soames left on Saturday, Mrs. Jones?'

'That's right, Superintendent. It was just before lunch. I remember it particularly because he asked if he could have something to eat a little earlier than usual. He said he had a train to catch.'

'Did he take a taxi?' Dwyer said hopefully.

'There's an Underground station at the end of the road. It's quicker than a taxi these days, traffic being what it is.'

'And Soames gave you no hint at all as to his destination?'

She shook her head. 'Just said he was taking a little business trip. That he'd probably be away for a week or ten days.'

'Has he done this sort of thing before?'

'Oh, yes, often.'

'And he never leaves you a forwarding address for urgent mail and so on?'

'I asked him about that once, but he said there was no point, that he would be on the move the whole time.'

'What about his social life? Did he have many callers?'

'None at all. He once told me that he preferred to keep his business and private life completely separate. He was a quiet, well-mannered person who kept himself to himself. Most evenings, he took a walk down to the George on the corner for a drink, but he never stayed for more than half an hour. He was fond of television and he looked after the garden for me. He was very good with flowers.'

'What about mail? Did he get much?'

She shrugged. 'Two or three letters a day, mostly circulars and so on.'

'Anything particularly interesting?'

She bridled at once. 'I've better things to do, Super-

105

intendent, than to go through my guests' mail.'

'I wasn't suggesting that you had been snooping, Mrs. Jones,' Vanbrugh said patiently. 'But quite obviously, you must sort the mail every morning after it's been delivered. It would be only natural for an intelligent person to notice anything unusual, any change in the pattern.'

She responded immediately, almost as a reflex action. 'It's funny you should say that. Nearly all Mr. Soames' letters used to come from the London area, but during the past few weeks they've been coming from all over the place.'

'Can you remember where?'

'He had a couple from Manchester and several from the Lake District. The day he left, he had one from Taunton. That's in the West Country,' she added. 'I spent my holidays near there last year.'

Dwyer had taken a sudden, involuntary step forward, but Vanbrugh stilled him with a quick gesture from one hand. 'These letters from the Lake District, Mrs. Jones, can you remember where they were from?'

'Oh, yes,' she said, 'because he always replied within a day or two. Sometimes I posted the letters for him. Kendal, that was the place. He used to write to a Mr. Grant at Kendal.'

'And you can't remember the address?'

She shook her head. 'I'm afraid not. It was addressed care of somebody else, I do know that. I always assumed it was a boarding house or something similar.' She patted her hair impatiently. 'You know there's really nothing more I can tell you, Superintendent.'

Vanbrugh gave her his most charming smile. 'My dear Mrs. Jones, you've helped us more than you'll ever know. I don't think we'll need to trouble you again.'

He went down the stairs quickly, Dwyer at his heels, opened the front door and went down the path. Scott was waiting for them. 'Any luck, sir?'

'You could say that.' Vanbrugh turned to Dwyer. 'An

interesting coincidence, isn't it, Soames and Pope being in touch with someone in the Lake District.'

'But what on earth would they be doing there, sir?' Dwyer said. 'It doesn't make sense.'

'Oh, I don't know,' Vanbrugh said. 'It's remote, secluded and they'll pretty well have the place to themselves at this time of the year.'

'If they *are* there, sir,' Dwyer reminded him.

Vanbrugh grinned. 'When you've been at this game as long as I have, Sergeant, you'll learn an interesting fact. That police work is mainly a matter of rather tedious routine, of question and answer, of sitting back, assessing the facts and looking for a pattern.'

'I know that much already, sir.'

'But that's not all,' Vanbrugh went on. 'As the years pass you'll find you develop a sort of extra faculty, an instinct that tells you a thing's so, even when you can't actually prove it. It's a good copper's most valuable asset.' He took out his pipe and gripped it firmly between his teeth. 'Soames and Pope are either in Kendal or somewhere near,' he said. 'I've never been so sure of anything in my life.'

'And Rogan, sir?'

Vanbrugh shook his head and some of the excitement died in him. 'Now there you have me. The trouble is, it doesn't make any kind of sense. Neither does the fact that he's mixed up with a couple of villains like Soames and Pope. They're just not his style.'

'What's the next move, sir?'

'Straight to the Yard. I'll see the Assistant Commissioner and make arrangements for us to leave for the Lake District at once. I'll get him to fix up full co-operation for us with the County Constabulary.'

'We won't reach Kendal before nine or ten tonight, sir,' Dwyer pointed out. 'We wouldn't do much till tomorrow.'

'You said Soames was nicked in 1958, didn't you?' Vanbrugh demanded. 'The least you can do is get his picture from records and wire it to Kendal together with that one of Pope. The sooner we get the local men looking out for them, the better. And we'll need the County Constabulary in on this, too.'

As the car moved away, he sank back against the padded seat, no longer tired, a hollow ache of excitement in the pit of his stomach. He was as certain as he had ever been about anything, that the answer to this whole affair lay in the last place in the country he would ever have thought of looking.

At that precise moment, Soames was crouched in a clump of bushes at the side of the coast road a few yards away from the signpost indicating the way to Marsh-End.

The small green saloon he had hired from a garage in Broughton-in-Furness was parked in a clearing to the rear. The fact that he was here at all was purely accidental. He had been waiting at the side of the Ambleside road for Pope who had gone up the valley on foot to keep a prearranged appointment with Morgan, when the shooting brake containing Rogan and Hannah Costello had come down from Scardale. Soames, his cunning mind working overtime, had simply seized the opportunity.

Rogan was not expecting to be followed. His decision to make a last visit to Colum O'More had been taken at a moment's notice, mainly because he had wanted to be alone with Hannah and in any case, he carried the keys of the cattle truck and the Morris van in his pocket.

They chose the long way round through Hawkshead, Coniston and Broughton and there was a fair amount of traffic on the road, which was greatly to Soames' advantage.

Cautious by nature, he was anything but a violent man and he knew just when it paid to take a chance and when it did not. When the shooting brake took the turning for Marsh-End he drove by, then turned and quickly found somewhere to park. Then he moved cautiously through the trees until he came upon the farm and the brake parked in the yard. He returned to the main road at once and took up his position in the shelter of some bushes.

The rain continued to fall steadily during the hours that he waited, but finally the brake reappeared and he drew back into the bushes until the sound of its engine faded into the distance.

He left his car where it was and moved back through the trees towards the farm. There was no sign of life anywhere and he stood at the edge of the yard examining the windows for a moment, then crossed to the door.

It opened to his touch and he walked softly along the whitewashed passage. The living room door was slightly ajar and someone coughed. He pushed the door open and stepped in.

Colum O'More was sitting by the fire in the act of applying a match to the bowl of his pipe. He stared at Soames as if he had seen a ghost and a quick anger kindled in his eyes.

'What the devil are you doing here?'

'I thought it was time we had a little chat, Mr. O'More.' Soames moved forward, shook the rain from his hat and placed it carefully on the table.

'I've nothing to say to you,' O'More said. 'You've been paid for what you've done, well paid and there's an end to it.'

'I have a friend in Dublin, Mr. O'More, did you know that?' Soames held his hands out to the fire. 'He's been making a few enquiries for me. Among the right people, you understand.' He smiled gently. 'The headquarters of your movement in Dublin, or what's left of it, don't seem to have heard from you in five years or more.' He shook his head reprovingly. 'You've not been telling the truth, Mr. O'More. I wonder what Sean Rogan would say to that?'

CHAPTER FOURTEEN

A COLD wind slanting across the square drove rain against the window with the force of lead shot as Vanbrugh stared morosely into the street. Already half-convinced that he was wrong, an abortive morning spent visiting every hotel in Kendal without finding a trace of either Soames or Pope, hadn't improved his temper. He wondered impatiently what was keeping Dwyer.

There was a knock on the door and a young constable entered with a cup of tea. As he turned to leave, Dwyer came in.

'You can make that two.' He shook rain from his hat and unbuttoned his coat. 'What a climate.'

'Any luck?' Vanbrugh demanded.

Dwyer shook his head. 'We've visited every guest-house and boarding house in Kendal without a trace. I've told the men to get some lunch and report back in an hour.'

'I didn't do any better at the hotels.'

The young constable brought in another cup of tea and Dwyer sipped it gratefully. 'Of course, there must be a lot of people in a place like this who take in paying guests, especially in the season.'

'Too many,' Vanbrugh said. 'It would take a house-to-house search to find them all. We simply haven't the men or the time.'

'It would explain the bit about this bloke Grant's address being care-of-someone else.'

'I've been in touch with the local Postmaster about that,' Vanbrugh said. 'I know it's a long shot that a postman might remember something like that. I know from past experience that most of these fellows get to know their round very well.'

'Any joy?'

'Not yet. Most of the men are still due-in from the lunchtime delivery. He's going to see them all before they go off duty and give me a ring.' He glanced at his watch. 'Two o'clock. That gives us half an hour.'

'There's a pub just round the corner,' Dwyer said. 'We could probably get some sandwiches or a pork pie or something.'

'Something like a pint, you mean?'

'It's been a hard morning, sir.'

Vanbrugh grinned and took down his coat from behind the door. 'Well, if you're paying, Sergeant....'

Looking over Hannah's shoulders through the flooded windscreen, Rogan could see Paddy Costello several hundred yards ahead, standing at the side of the road. The small man clambered into the passenger seat and closed the door with a curse.

'Christ Jesus, but I'm soaked to the bloody skin. It cuts into you like razor blades, that stuff.'

'Everything go off all right?' Rogan said.

'I parked it at the back of that ruined barn. Sure and there won't be a soul about on a day like this.'

Rogan eased back against the side of the van and lit a cigarette. He tossed the packet across to Fletcher who sat opposite, strangely formal in his navy blue uniform. The big man extracted a cigarette with hands that shook slightly.

'What's wrong with you?' Morgan demanded. 'Wetting yourself?'

'Why don't you get stuffed?' Fletcher leaned back and blew out a cloud of smoke with evident satisfaction. 'It's going to be all right, I can tell.'

'What did you do, write to Gypsy Rose?' Morgan asked sarcastically.

Fletcher turned, one gnarled fist balling and Rogan cut in sharply, 'Knock it off. You can cut pieces out of each other from tomorrow on as far as I'm concerned. Until then, I'm in charge.'

A few minutes later, they started to move through Kendal and he glanced at his watch. 'A quarter of an hour.'

He could see beads of sweat lining the folds of skin that draped over the back of Costello's collar and the old man pulled down his cap with a hand that shook slightly. Fletcher showed no apparent emotion and Morgan grinned.

'Nothing quite like it, is there?'

Rogan didn't reply, but he knew exactly what the man was getting at. The hollowness in the stomach, the tightness in the chest, the difficulty in breathing properly. It wasn't fear exactly, but something rather more subtle. A strange mixture of excitement and apprehension. A feeling he had known many times before that lasted until the exact moment that you made your first decisive move. After that, there was never time to think of anything but the job in hand.

The van moved along the narrow lane between high hedges and then, quite suddenly, they were turning into the parking space outside Rigg Station. Hannah braked to a halt, and reversed in one smooth motion until the back of the van was no more than a foot from the loading bay. Rogan opened the door, stepped out and moved into the booking hall.

A silk scarf was already knotted at the back of his neck and he pulled it over the lower half of his face and jerked down the peak of his old tweed cap. He opened the door of the stationmaster's office and stepped inside.

Briggs stood at the fireplace, one hand reaching for the kettle, a pint pot in the other. He started to turn and Rogan took the Colt automatic from his pocket.

The old man's face was a study in bewilderment. He opened his mouth as if to speak and his jaw went slack as the shock of what was happening hit him with the force of a physical blow.

Paddy Costello moved inside quickly, opened the other door and passed into the baggage hall. As Rogan heard the outer doors open, he said to Briggs, 'Do as you're told and you won't get hurt. Take off your cap, jacket and waistcoat and put them on the desk.'

The old man stood there staring at him, frozen by fear, his mouth open. Rogan stepped forward in one quick movement and touched him between the eyes with the cold barrel of the automatic.

'Now, not tomorrow.'

His action had exactly the psychological effect that he had hoped. Briggs put his pint pot on the mantelpiece and hurriedly took off his jacket. When Costello came back into the office, Briggs was standing by the fireplace, his shirt sleeves rolled above the elbow, one arm only half the thickness of the other, badly disfigured by the jagged distinctive scars of old shrapnel wounds.

'Where did you pick that lot up?' Rogan asked.

Briggs seemed to come to life a little and his head went back. 'The Somme, 1916.'

'If you got through that bloody lot, you'll survive anything. Lie on the floor and close your eyes.'

He nodded to Costello who moved forward quickly, a coil of rope in his hands. Rogan went into the baggage hall. Outside, the wheels of the old Morris van skidded on the loose gravel as Hannah drove away. Fletcher dragged in the fourth mailbag and Morgan closed the door.

He turned to Rogan, the skin drawn tightly across his cheekbones, eyes very bright. 'Everything okay?'

Rogan nodded and glanced at his watch. 'Five minutes, maybe sooner.'

Costello had knotted a scarf around the old man's eyes and gagged him with a piece of sticking plaster. He was tying his wrists behind him as Rogan went back into the office and the Irishman nudged him with the toe of his shoe.

'I'll finish that, you get changed.'

As Costello hurriedly took off his raincoat and pulled on the uniform waistcoat, Rogan dropped to one knee and lashed the old man's wrists together, securely, but not too tightly.

He patted Briggs on the shoulder. 'I'm putting you out of harm's way for a little while. Don't try anything silly and you'll be all right. Understand?'

The old man nodded and Rogan opened the door to the washroom, picked him up and carried him inside. He laid him on the floor, went back into the office and closed the door.

Costello buttoned his jacket and put on the cap. He examined himself in the cracked mirror over the fire, turned and laughed nervously. 'Will I do?'

'Perfect!' Rogan said. 'Now get out on that platform and look busy.'

He stood at the narrow window watching Costello go to work with his broom, then went back into the baggage hall. Morgan had one of the double doors open slightly and was looking outside. He made a sudden, cutting gesture with one hand as Fletcher started to speak and, through the heavy rain, they heard the sound of an engine approaching.

Rogan moved beside him. As he peered through the narrow crack, the van turned off the road on to the parking space. It seemed strangely ordinary, its coachwork painted dark blue with no distinguishing characteristics except for the circular aerial on the roof.

It rolled to a halt a few yards away, giving him a clear view of the two occupants. The driver looked like an ex-Guards N.C.O., dark moustache bristling beneath the gold-rimmed peaked cap. The guard was a younger man with a hard, bony face and a scar bisecting one cheek.

Rogan saw him yawn and pick up the radio telephone receiver. A moment later he started to speak. He replaced the receiver, put a cigarette in his mouth and reached across to the watch held out to him by the driver.

The door leading to the platform opened and Costello hurried in.

'It's coming.'

'All right. Get outside and give them a nod,' Rogan said.

Costello hesitated and Morgan kicked him viciously on the leg. 'Get moving, damn you!'

Costello opened the door, leaned out and raised a hand. The driver of the van nodded, turned in a half-circle and started to reverse.

Rogan could hear the train beginning to slow on the run in to the station and he gave Costello a shove across the baggage hall. 'On the platform and stay by the door.'

Rogan stepped back into the office leaving the other two waiting in the baggage hall. Morgan stood in one corner by the double doors, Fletcher in the other, each of them with a rubber truncheon ready in his right hand.

Then everything seemed to be happening at once. As the noise of the train filled the building, the double doors were pushed open, hiding Fletcher and Morgan from view. The driver came in first, a receipt book in one hand, dragging a mailbag behind him. The guard followed with another, cigarette still dangling from one corner of his mouth.

The doors swung back and Morgan and Fletcher moved in together, truncheons flailing down expertly. The driver dropped like a sack, unconscious from the first devastating blow. The younger man managed to turn, dropping his mailbag and reached for his own truncheon. His mouth opened in a soundless cry, drowned by the noise of the engine and Fletcher slashed him across the edge of the neck.

Rogan moved in fast, grabbed the driver's feet and dragged him into the office. As he dropped him behind the desk out of sight from the window, Fletcher followed with the other guard.

Rogan moved back into the baggage hall and Morgan came in from the ramp, the driver's gold peaked cap slanting across his eyes. 'The bloody van's empty. Only the two bags.'

So Colum O'More had been wrong for once, but there

was no time to worry about that now. Rogan was already on one knee beside the two mailbags, a pair of pliers in his hand. Each bag was fastened by heavy wire, an official lead seal inscribed with several code words and a number. He snipped the wire and quickly laced it through the metal eyelet holes of one of the dummy bags which Fletcher dragged forward. He joined the broken ends of the wire as neatly as possible, twisting them together, then pushed the join out of sight through one of the eyelet holes in the mouth of the bag.

As he repeated the operation on the other, Morgan dropped to one knee beside him. 'Let's hope they don't check those too carefully.'

'Why should they?' Rogan said calmly and got to his feet. 'Out you go.'

The young guard's cap was a size too small for Fletcher, but he tilted it forward over his eyes and lifted up a mailbag. Morgan picked up the receipt book and the other bag and moved to the end of the baggage hall. He hesitated, opened the door and moved out. Rogan held his breath and waited.

It was strangely quiet on the platform, the muffled rumble of the diesel engines the only sound. Paddy Costello leaned on his broom by the door, making a great show of examining his watch, and the sliding door of the mail van stood open.

Morgan moved forward and an attendant leaned out and grinned. 'Aren't you beggars ever late?'

'Don't ask me,' Morgan said. 'First time we've done this run.'

He heaved his mailbag into the van and Fletcher followed suit. The attendant produced a pen and held out his hand. 'Let's have it.'

Morgan opened the receipt book and handed it to him. The attendant signed the top copy, tore it off and handed the book back. 'That's it then.'

He started to draw back and Morgan said, 'Christ, I was forgetting. Do me a favour, mate. I gave the radio a bit of a bash getting out of the cab and it's on the blink. Give 'em a ring at headquarters, will you, and tell 'em we're on our way in?'

'Anything to oblige.'

It was as simple as that. The sliding door closed and Costello raised a hand to the guard who leaned out of his window at the rear of the train. A whistle sounded faintly and, in a moment, the great diesel engines picked up and the train slid away.

As the rear of the train disappeared into the heavy rain, the three men crowded into the baggage hall excitedly. 'We made it, by Christ! We made it!' Fletcher said.

'A long way to go yet,' Rogan told him. 'Get those two mailbags into the van and don't forget the dummies. Don't leave them anything they might be able to trace.' He turned to Morgan. 'You help me in here.'

The van driver and his guard still lay unconscious by the desk and Rogan examined them. There was a trickle of blood at the back of the driver's ear and he looked up at Morgan grimly.

'You don't pull your punches.'

Morgan shrugged. 'I could never see the point.'

Rogan produced a couple of lengths of thin cord from his pocket and they quickly tied the wrists of the two unconscious men behind them.

'Right, into the van and get that engine started,' Rogan said. 'I'll be out in a minute.'

He opened the washroom door and dropped to one knee beside Briggs. The old man was breathing heavily through the nose and Rogan pulled the sticking plaster away from his mouth. Briggs sucked in a lungful of air gratefully and Rogan patted him on the shoulder.

'You'll be all right, Dad. That goods train should arrive in exactly twenty-five minutes.'

The old man turned his head blindly towards him. 'God help you, lad, because you'll never get away with this.'

'You take a chance every day of your life.' Rogan hurried out through the baggage hall. The rear door of the van stood open, Costello peering out. Rogan stepped inside and closed the door and Morgan turned from the small armoured glass window and gunned the motor.

As the van moved at high speed along the narrow lane between the hedges, Rogan flicked the switch of the inter-communication system.

'Take it easy, especially on the way through Kendal. We've all the time in the world.'

'What kind of a steamer do you think I am?' Morgan said angrily, all the tension of the past ten minutes burst-ing out of him.

Rogan flicked the switch and sat down. Paddy Costello was slumped on the bench seat opposite, his face shining with sweat, hands grasped tightly together.

'It's going to be fine,' Rogan said. 'Everything's going to be all right.'

The old man nodded, lips compressed together as if he couldn't trust himself to speak. In Kendal, traffic was light and Morgan had to stop only twice at traffic lights. Once through the town and on to the Windermere road, he increased speed and turned into the plantation of fir exactly eight minutes after leaving Rigg Station.

As the van braked to a halt, Rogan opened the door and jumped out. Hannah was standing beside the cattle truck and she came forward anxiously.

'Everything all right?'

Rogan nodded. 'Couldn't have gone better. What about the Morris?'

'Parked at the back of the barn.'

Costello and Fletcher were already transferring the mailbags from the armoured van to the cattle truck and Morgan leaned out of the driver's window and watched. Fletcher gave him a shout and Morgan released the handbrake and took the van towards the rim of the flooded gravel pits, where he jumped clear. A second later, the van plunged over the edge. By the time Rogan and Hannah had joined him, it had already disappeared.

'Now the Morris,' Rogan said. 'We'd better shove her over a little further up.'

They ran the little van along the track which followed the edge of the pits and, as it dipped over the crown of a small rise, Rogan gave the wheel a twist and jumped back. The van, running on down the slope, veered sharply to the left and vanished over the edge.

Costello was already behind the wheel of the cattle truck, Hannah beside him in the cab. As the engine roared into life, Rogan and Morgan joined Fletcher in the back. The truck dipped over the rutted surface of the track, paused for a moment outside the gate while Hannah closed it, then turned into the main road and moved rapidly towards Windermere.

'How are we off for time?' Morgan demanded.

Rogan checked his watch. 'That goods train is due in at Rigg in exactly twelve minutes if it's on time.'

'Which they never are.'

'It'll take the crew at least five minutes to sort out what's happened and get in touch with the authorities, another ten for the police to get any kind of an alert out. That gives us at least twenty-seven minutes.'

'And Ambleside's only ten miles away.' Morgan laughed harshly. 'We're home and dry.'

Fletcher, sitting against one side of the truck, nudged a mailbag with the toe of his shoe. 'My God, but I'd like to know what's inside those two babies.'

'I should be able to tell you,' Morgan said. 'I haven't had time to look before.'

He took the receipt book from the pocket of his uniform and opened it quickly. 'It's headed "Consignment for pulping".'

'That means it's all old stuff,' Fletcher said. 'Just the job.'

'Bag Rs3, forty-five thousand in one pound notes, twenty-five thousand in fivers. Bag Rs4, fifty thousand in one pound notes, twenty in fivers.'

'Christ Jesus,' Fletcher whispered. 'That's a hundred and forty thousand quid in old notes.'

'Not bad,' Morgan said. 'Split three ways, that's better than forty grand apiece.' He grinned. 'An interesting thought.'

'Come on, let's have a look,' Fletcher said excitedly and reached for one of the bags. Rogan slammed the heel of his shoe across the back of the outstretched hand.

Fletcher scrambled to one knee, snarling like an animal and found himself looking into the barrel of the Colt automatic. 'Colum O'More opens those bags, no one else.' Rogan reached forward and touched Fletcher between the eyes with the barrel. 'Another play like that and I'll kill you. That's a promise.'

CHAPTER FIFTEEN

THE parking space outside Rigg Station was more crowded than it had probably ever been in its previous existence, and as Vanbrugh moved to the edge of the ramp another patrol car rolled to a halt.

A couple of ambulance attendants came out of the baggage hall carrying the driver of the armoured van on a stretcher and two more followed with the guard. Vanbrugh opened his tobacco pouch and filled his pipe as he watched them place the injured men in the ambulance and drive away.

By sheer chance, he and Dwyer had been in conference with a Superintendent Gregory of the County Constabulary at Kendal police headquarters, discussing their abortive visit to the G.P.O., when the alarm had come through from Rigg. Vanbrugh, drawn by a more than professional interest, had accompanied Gregory at once.

As he applied a match to his pipe, Dwyer moved out of the baggage hall. 'It took nerve. You've got to give them that. Of all the bloody cheek. Imagine getting the train to phone in for them.'

'A touch of genius,' Vanbrugh said.

Dwyer appeared to hesitate and then continued, 'It's a familiar pattern, somehow, don't you think so, sir?'

Vanbrugh sighed heavily. 'Strange that I should have told you about that business in France during the war only the other day. This affair's been almost a carbon copy.'

Gregory joined them, a tall, spare man in a beautifully tailored uniform. 'I've been thinking, sir,' he said to Vanbrugh. 'This has been a big city job, no doubt about that. Any chance of your man Rogan being involved?'

'Every chance, I'm afraid,' Vanbrugh said. 'Mind if I have a word with the stationmaster?'

'Help yourself.'

They went into the office where old Briggs sat at his desk, a cup of tea held in both hands. A constable stood at the door and a sergeant sat on the edge of the desk, taking Briggs' statement. He stood to one side and Gregory smiled down at the old man.

'Feeling a little better, Mr. Briggs?'

'Nothing wrong with me that a couple of rums won't cure,' the old man said.

'This is Chief Superintendent Vanbrugh of Scotland Yard. He'd like to ask you a few questions.'

Vanbrugh was reading quickly through the Sergeant's notebook and he nodded and looked up. 'You say here that you never got a look at the face of the man with the gun?'

'Couldn't do. He was wearing a scarf.'

'He was a big man?'

'A giant, leastways, that's the way he looked to me.'

Vanbrugh nodded. 'What about his voice?'

'Well-spoken, an educated bloke.'

'Could he have been Irish?'

'It's possible. Irish or Scots, I wouldn't like to say which. To tell you the truth, he wasn't such a bad bloke.'

'What makes you say that?'

The old man held up his crippled arm. 'He asked me how I got that. When I told him the Somme, he laughed and said if I could get through that lot, I could survive anything. Another thing, he took the time to come back to the washroom afterwards to pull off my gag. I was near choking.'

Vanbrugh turned and nodded to Gregory. 'Rogan, without a doubt.' They moved out through the baggage hall to the ramp and he slammed a fist into the palm of his other hand. 'But why? It just isn't in character. I've known Sean Rogan for years. He isn't the type.'

'He's been inside a long time, sir,' Dwyer said gently. 'People change.'

Before Vanbrugh could reply, a police constable leaned out of the window of a patrol car and called, 'Superintendent Gregory. Message from Kendal.'

Gregory jumped to the ground and walked briskly to the car. He leaned in the window and Vanbrugh watched him take the receiver the constable offered him. A moment later, he straightened excitedly.

'That accommodation address you wanted,' he called to Vanbrugh. 'They've traced a postman who thinks he knows it. He's been off duty for a couple of days with a sprained ankle. That's why they didn't come up with him earlier.'

Vanbrugh jumped to the ground and moved forward quickly. 'You know what this could mean?'

'Don't I just.' Gregory smiled coolly. 'I'm afraid someone may be in for a rather nasty surprise.'

The address was that of a small back-street newsagent in Kendal and a patrol car was waiting when Gregory and the two Scotland Yard men arrived. The postman, a man named Harvey, was sitting in the back, a walking stick between his knees, chatting to the patrol car crew.

When Gregory leaned in the window, the two constables got out of the car at once. 'Mr. Harvey—I'm Superintendent Gregory, County Constabulary. You're sure about this?'

'About the letters addressed to Charles Grant, care of Tomlinson's? Oh, yes, sir. I remember kidding him about it and him saying how trade was bad and who was he to turn down ten bob a week just to accept delivery of a few letters.'

Gregory straightened and turned to the two constables. 'Have you been in?'

'Not yet, sir.'

He nodded to Vanbrugh. 'After you.'

Tomlinson was a middle-aged man with greying hair and horn-rimmed spectacles that had been badly repaired with electrician's tape. When they went in he was standing behind the counter, leaning forward to see what all the fuss was about.

'Mr. Tomlinson?' Gregory said. 'I'm Superintendent Gregory, County Constabulary. This is Chief Superintendent Vanbrugh and Sergeant Dwyer of Scotland Yard. We understand you might be able to help us in an investigation we're conducting.'

Tomlinson looked completely bewildered. 'I don't even know what you're talking about.'

'You've been allowing this address to be used by a Mr. Charles Grant, isn't that so?'

Tomlinson nodded, a slight frown knitting his brow. 'Nothing wrong in that, is there?'

'We think Mr. Grant may be a man we're looking for. Have you any idea as to his present whereabouts?'

'Not a clue,' Tomlinson said. 'I've only ever seen him once, that was the first time he came in. He was pretty old, walked with a stick. Irish, I think, which surprised me, him having a Scots name.'

'Have many letters come for him?'

Tomlinson nodded. 'Three or four a week, I'd say. They've been picked up by a young woman as a rule.

She's usually looked in most afternoons.'

'Do you know her name?'

Tomlinson shook his head. 'No, but I've seen her at Ambleside Market a couple of times. She was with an old fella called Costello—Paddy Costello. Runs an excuse for a sheep farm up Scardale way. Big boozer and gambler. He's known in every pub in the district.'

Gregory was already moving outside. He leaned in the window of his car and said to the driver, 'Get through to H.Q. at once. Tell them to phone the Station Sergeant at Ambleside. Ask him what he knows about a man called Paddy Costello who keeps a farm somewhere Scardale way. And tell them this is top priority.'

He turned and took out a silver case as Vanbrugh and Dwyer joined him. 'From the sound of things, this could be it.'

He offered Vanbrugh a cigarette and they stood there smoking nervously, neither man speaking. Within an incredibly short space of time, Gregory's driver leaned out of the window.

'On Costello, sir. Station Sergeant at Ambleside knows him well. A list of drunk and disorderly charges as long as your arm. Keeps a farm at the top end of Scardale below the old mine workings.'

'Does he live alone?'

'He has a son and his niece has been living with him for the past ten months. Hannah Maria Costello. She has a record, sir. Six months at Holloway on a vice charge last year.'

Gregory turned to Vanbrugh. 'Rather more than promising, I'd say.'

The driver interrupted. 'One more thing, sir. This man Soames that Chief Superintendent Vanbrugh wanted to see, they've picked him up in Broughton. They want to know what to do with him.'

'We've more important business in hand,' Vanbrugh said. 'Tell them to run him up to Kendal. I'll see him later.' He turned to Gregory, his face expressionless. 'I'd say we could do with a couple of dozen good men.'

'Don't worry, sir.' Gregory smiled gently. 'We breed them on the large side up here. Your pal Rogan may be in for something of a shock.'

CHAPTER SIXTEEN

When they reached Scardale, Costello drove the truck straight into the barn and parked it behind the shooting brake. When he cut the engine, Rogan jumped to the ground and nodded to Morgan and Fletcher.

'Inside, you two, and stay there.'

As Hannah and Costello came round from the cab, Fletcher said, 'What the hell do you mean, inside? I've just about had enough of you and your bleeding orders.'

He came forward with a rush. Rogan waited till he was close, then pulled out his automatic and struck him heavily across the face.

As the steel sight on the end of the barrel sliced across his cheek, Fletcher gave a cry of agony, hands going to his face as blood spurted.

'You wait, you bastard,' he said through clenched teeth. 'I'll fix you. I'll fix you good.'

Rogan looked at Morgan coldly. 'Any questions?'

Morgan shrugged. 'You're the boss.'

Fletcher stumbled out of the barn and Morgan followed him. Rogan held out his hand to Costello.

'I'll take the truck keys.'

Costello handed them over hastily. 'Do you want me inside with the others?'

'For the time being.'

The old man went across the yard and Hannah pulled

off her scarf and shook her hair free. 'You're harder than I ever thought you could be.'

'With scum like that, it pays.' He took her hand and pulled her close for a moment. 'How do you feel?'

'How am I supposed to feel?' She shrugged. 'Tired, washed out. I could sleep for a week.'

'What you need is a cup of tea with a drop of the right stuff in it and something to eat.'

She smiled wanly. 'Maybe you're right. What about you?'

'I'll be in later. Something I want to do here first.'

He pulled her into his arms and kissed her briefly and fine straw dust drifted down through the cracks in the loft above. When they looked up, they saw Brendan peering over the edge.

He dropped to the ground and scrambled to his feet, white with excitement. He tried to speak, his mouth opening and closing, but nothing emerged and Hannah put her hands on his shoulders.

'Take your time. Just take your time.'

The boy breathed in deeply and the words came out of him in a great rush. 'There's a man at the house. He came up the valley road just after you'd gone.'

'A big man with black hair?'

'That's right.'

'Jack Pope,' Rogan told Hannah.

'I think he was trying to find me,' the boy said. 'He looked everywhere, but I hid under the hay in the loft.'

Hannah looked at Rogan anxiously. 'What do you think they're up to?'

'I should have thought that was obvious.' He stood thinking, a slight frown on his face, then nodded. 'You go in and prepare a meal.' She opened her mouth to protest and he gave her a small push. 'Don't worry. I know what I'm doing.'

Fletcher sat on the edge of the kitchen table, cursing as Morgan fixed another large strip of sticking plaster across his cheek.

'Anybody'd think he had it in for you, Jesse,' Morgan said with a grin.

Fletcher cursed and snatched the tumbler into which Costello had just poured a generous measure of whisky. 'I'll fix that swine yet.'

'That'll be the day,' Morgan jeered.

He left them there and went along the passage to his bedroom. Rogan was tough all right and he'd be a hard nut to crack. But whatever happened, Morgan hadn't the slightest intention of allowing a hundred and forty thousand pounds to slip through his fingers without trying to do something about it.

He opened the bedroom door, turned to close it and found Jack Pope standing in the corner, a revolver in his right hand. The tension oozed out of Pope in a long sigh and he wiped sweat from his forehead.

'I thought it might be Rogan.'

'He's still in the barn,' Morgan said. 'Did you have any trouble getting in?'

'No, but I couldn't find the lad anywhere.'

'Not to worry. That kid wanders around all over the place.' Morgan pulled the revolver from Pope's grasp. 'Where did you get the shooter?'

'Soames picked it up in the Smoke. Thought it might come in useful.'

'Any spare slugs?'

'Half a dozen, that's all.' Pope handed them over. 'What was the take?'

'A hundred and forty thousand. Not as good as expected. There were only two mailbags.'

'And Rogan's got them?'

'That's it. Says he intends to hand them over to O'More intact.'

'I had a phone call from Soames last night,' Pope said. 'He's managed to trace O'More to a farm called Marsh-End. It's just off the coast road near Whitbeck.'

'Which means the old devil's probably got a boat all ready and waiting for a quick exit across the Irish Sea.'

'That's right. What's our next move?'

Morgan went to the door, opened it and called to Fletcher and Costello. They came in a moment later, Fletcher carrying the bottle of whisky in one hand and a tumbler in the other.

'So you got here?' he growled at Pope. 'A fat lot of bloody good it'll do you, the way things look at the moment.'

'I wouldn't be too sure.' Morgan held out the revolver in the palm of his hand. 'This might just even things up a little.'

'Saints preserve us,' Paddy Costello said.

'Have you still got that spare ignition key for the cattle truck?' Morgan demanded.

The old man produced it from one of his waistcoat pockets and handed it over. Morgan moved to the window, staying behind the curtains as Hannah came out of the barn and crossed to the front door. They heard it open and she passed along the passage to the kitchen. He moved to the door, listened for a second, then returned to the window. Brendan emerged from the barn pushing a hand cart loaded with several bulging sacks.

'What's the kid up to?' he demanded. 'I didn't even see him go in there.'

Paddy Costello joined him at the window. 'Never mind him. He creeps around like a flaming ghost.'

Brendan pushed the cart out through the main gate and turned up the track towards the mine workings. 'Where's he taking that little lot?' Fletcher said.

'We've got some sheep penned in the enclosure up at the village. The ones I'm supposed to drive in to Millom market tomorrow. He'll be taking them some feed.'

Rogan came out of the barn, a mailbag over each shoulder. He stood looking after the boy for a moment, then walked across to the house.

'Let's take him now on his way in,' Pope said.

Morgan shook his head, weighing the revolver in one hand. 'He's had a lot of shooting experience. I wouldn't like to be the one to try anything from the front. We'll bide our time.' He turned to Pope. 'You stay here. You two come with me.'

When Rogan came in they were in the living room, Morgan and Fletcher sitting on either side of the fire, Costello at the table.

The Irishman stood in the doorway, a mailbag in each hand, and looked at them calmly. Morgan could feel the revolver in his pocket and fought against the suicidal impulse to pull it out. There was a strange magnetism about Rogan, a sort of invulnerability that seemed to say that no one could ever touch him.

His ascendancy over the three of them was almost tangible as he tossed the two mailbags into a corner by the door and unbuttoned his raincoat.

'That kid of yours is beginning to give me the creeps,' he said to Costello. 'He was playing around in the hayloft back there in the barn. He'll never know how close he came to getting a bullet in him.'

'It's sorry I am to hear it, Mr. Rogan,' Costello said hastily. 'I'll boot the behind off him when he gets in.'

Hannah called from the kitchen and Rogan sniffed. 'Bacon frying or I miss my guess. Nothing like a job of work well done to give you an appetite. We'd better go in.'

'Not me,' Fletcher said and reached for the whisky bottle.

Rogan took a single pace forward and pulled the bottle from his hand. He put it down on the sideboard and turned, his face quite calm.

'I said we eat.'

Fletcher sat there glaring and Morgan slapped him on the shoulder. 'Come on, Jesse.'

Paddy Costello was already on his way and Fletcher followed. In the doorway, Morgan paused and turned. 'Sometimes you can push people just a little too hard. Ever thought of that?'

'You're a good talker,' Rogan said. 'Keep it up long

enough and you might convince yourself you could do something about me.'

Morgan's face turned very pale and all light died in his eyes. 'I did two years in a Chinese prison camp in Korea, Rogan, did you know that? When they released me, I had a double hernia from the number of times the guards had booted me in the crotch and T.B. in one lung.'

'So?' Rogan said.

'When I got home, I found that nobody gave a damn. They didn't seem to know a war had been going on.'

'What's that supposed to prove—that you had an excuse?'

Morgan laughed harshly. 'I haven't needed one since the day I was old enough to work out the odds in this lousy world for myself. I'll tell you one thing, friend. If I could survive those Chinese bastards, I can survive you. Just think about that.'

He went along the passage and Rogan smiled softly. Nothing like an open declaration of war to let you know where you stood. He hung his raincoat behind the door, took the Colt automatic from his pocket and pushed it down into his waistband at the rear so that it was covered by the tail of his jacket, the butt hard against the small of his back. He buttoned his jacket at the front and went along to the kitchen.

It was an uncomfortable meal and eaten in complete silence. Hannah moved from one to the other, refilling cups with fresh tea and bringing more bread from the dresser. On the occasions that she managed to catch Rogan's eye, her face was strained and anxious.

Finally, he pushed back his chair and said calmly, 'That'll do me for now. Let's go back to the living room.'

Fletcher looked angrily at Morgan who made a slight gesture with his head and stood up. Fletcher followed him out of the door, Costello trailing after them.

Hannah moved across to Rogan quickly. 'There's going to be trouble, Sean. I feel it.'

'Don't worry.' He smiled. 'I know what I'm doing. You

130

stay here.'

When he went into the living room, no one said a word. He picked up the bottle of whisky and a tumbler from the sideboard and sat on the edge of the table.

'Funny how you remember things. The last time I robbed a train was in France in '44. We had it all laid on to knock off one that was carrying a month's pay for a German Panzer Division. It would have been quite a haul.'

'What went wrong?' Morgan said.

'We never really found out. The important thing was that instead of the payroll, the train carried a company of German paratroops armed to the teeth and spoiling for action and let nobody kid you, those boys were good.'

'Somebody grassed?' Fletcher said, interested in spite of himself.

'One of three possibilities,' Rogan said. 'The first was a local farmer whose place we'd been using as headquarters for a while. He wet himself every time an ivy leaf tapped on the window.'

Costello flushed and looked away hurriedly and Rogan went on, 'Then there was a lovely specimen who'd been inside for just about every crime in the book. A big man at beating hell out of the prostitutes on the Marseilles waterfront when they objected to handing over half their takings.'

Fletcher's hand shook with rage as he raised his glass of whisky to his mouth and drained it and Morgan said calmly, 'What about the third?'

'He was the most dangerous of the lot. He'd even done three years in a Jesuit seminary training for the priesthood.' Rogan tapped his forehead. 'A hoodlum with brains. The worst kind there is. Pure evil.'

'Lucifer, Prince of Darkness. The fallen angel,' Morgan said. 'Now that, I find interesting. What happened?'

'We took them out into the forest, what was left of us, and shot them.'

'All three?'

'Nothing else to do under the circumstances.'

'Holy Mother,' Paddy Costello whispered in horror.

Rogan stuck a cigarette in the corner of his mouth and leaned down to light it with a splinter from the fire. In the brief moment that his back was turned, Morgan seized his chance, pulled out the revolver and extended his arm.

'I could blow your head off right now. Make a wrong move and I will.'

Rogan turned slowly, hands held well away from his body and Morgan called, 'Pope, get out here fast!'

There was a quick movement in the passage and Pope appeared in the doorway. 'What's going on?'

'Hello, Jack,' Rogan said. 'Fancy meeting you here?'

'Get a grip on those two mailbags,' Morgan said, 'and don't let them out of your sight. Jesse, get his gun.'

Fletcher came forward slowly, his ugly face splitting into a delighted grin. He stood looking at Rogan for a long moment and then quickly searched him. He frowned and turned.

'He hasn't got it on him.'

'That doesn't make sense,' Morgan said, suddenly wary. 'Look again, but watch him. He's a foxy bastard.'

'We can soon take care of that,' Fletcher said.

He turned back to Rogan and his fist swung in a short arc, catching the Irishman on the right cheek. Rogan rode the punch, allowing himself to stagger back. He went over the armchair, landing on his shoulders and pulled the automatic free at the same moment. He loosed off one quick shot that chipped splinters from the table and Morgan gave a cry of alarm.

'Get out of it, quick!'

He fired hastily and Rogan rolled for the shelter of the old horsehair sofa that stood against the wall. As he reached it, Morgan pushed Fletcher and Pope into the passage.

Rogan fired through the door, the bullet tearing its way through the flimsy woodwork and ricocheting be-

132

tween the stone walls of the passage.

Costello gave a cry of alarm, ran to the front door and wrenched it open and Pope went after him, the mailbags banging against his knees.

Morgan gave Fletcher a shove. 'Get after them, Jesse. We'll have to make a run for it in the truck.'

He fired through the door into the living room, keeping his back flat against the wall, then turned and ran after Fletcher. The big man was halfway across the yard and Pope and Costello were already vanishing through the open double doors into the half darkness.

As Morgan started to run a chair came through the window behind him. He turned and fired a wild shot that chipped stone from the wall ten feet off target, then ran, zig-zagging from side to side. A single shot chased him into the barn, ploughing into a bale of hay at the rear.

Fletcher and Pope had already got the mailbags into the back of the cattle truck and Morgan shoved Costello up behind the wheel. He followed him into the cab, pushed in the ignition key and switched on.

'Get this bloody thing moving.'

The old man's face was grey with fear and spittle dribbled from the corner of his mouth. Morgan slapped him heavily across the face. 'Get moving,' he cried.

Rogan was halfway across the yard and he dropped to one knee behind the water trough, aimed carefully and fired. As Morgan and Costello ducked, the bullet drilled a neat hole through the windscreen. Costello gave a cry of fear. He pressed the starter and slammed the stick into first gear.

The old cattle truck roared through the entrance, knocking one of the half-open doors off its hinges and they bounced over the potholes towards the gateway. Morgan fired in the general direction of the water trough to keep Rogan's head down and then they were through with a crunch of metal as the right wing crumpled against one of the stone gateposts.

Costello changed into top gear and rammed his foot hard against the boards, his hands tight on the wheel and Morgan looked back and laughed harshly as Rogan came through the gateway and started to run down the road after them.

'A fat lot of bloody good that'll do you.'

As he turned, putting the revolver into his pocket, the truck swung round the shoulder of the mountain and his throat went dry. A police car was moving towards them, at least half a dozen other vehicles strung out behind it.

Costello gave a hoarse cry and the police car slowed to a halt, turning broadside to block the narrow road. 'Brake, you stupid sod! Brake!' Morgan cried.

Costello seemed to lose all control. When he rammed down his foot, it caught the accelerator instead of the brake pedal and the truck shot forward. Its offside wheels ploughed into the rain-soaked grass shoulder and the wheel spun in his hands. Morgan had one quick glimpse of the steep slope dropping a hundred and fifty feet to the boulders in the stream below and his hand grabbed for the door handle. He jumped as the truck started to go over and the door swung back behind him, smashing Costello in the face as the old man tried to follow.

Morgan somersaulted twenty feet down the slope, coming to rest against a gorse bush. As he picked himself up the cattle truck bounced against a rock shelf fifty feet below. It soared into space, turning over almost in slow motion and Fletcher was tossed out, arms and legs flailing wildly.

The truck landed upside down in the stream bed with a terrible, grating crunch, and Fletcher landed on top of it. The petrol tank exploded immediately like a bomb, and orange and yellow flames lifted into the rain.

Morgan scrambled up the slope. He was badly shaken and blood poured down his face from a gash above his right eye, but the instinct for survival was strong. As he crossed the road he heard voices and turned to see several uniformed policemen running towards him. He fired and one of them seemed to trip and fall headlong. The others immediately scattered and Morgan ran for the shelter of a shallow ravine and followed its course up the side of the mountain.

Rogan had stopped running and was on his way back to the farm when he heard the first terrible crunch of metal as the truck went over the edge. He started to run back as the petrol tank exploded, and reached the point where the road curved round the shoulder of the mountain as Morgan fired at the police and staggered across.

A police car roared along the road and slewed broadside to protect the constable who had been shot. A large, heavily built man in a fawn trenchcoat jumped out and ran, crouching, to drop to one knee beside him.

Rogan recognized Dick Vanbrugh at once. The strange thing was his own lack of surprise, but he didn't stop to analyse that. He turned and ran back towards the farm. Hannah was standing in the gateway as he entered the yard.

'What is it? What's happened?'

'No time for questions. Grab your coat and get back out of here fast. We're leaving. I've still got a key for the shooting brake, remember?'

When he drove out of the barn, she was pulling on her sheepskin coat by the water trough. He opened the door and she scrambled in and slammed it as they drove away.

When they moved through the gate and turned left towards the head of the valley, she touched his arm. 'Where are we going?'

'Through the Long Cut, Brendan's waiting up there now with the mailbags. The two I brought into the house were the dummies.'

'What about the others? What happened back there?'

'The whole place is crawling with peelers. The truck went over the edge of the road.'

Her face was very white. 'And my uncle?'

135

'It went up like a torch.'

She turned away, crossing herself automatically. He reached out and took her hand and she held it tightly as they went over the brow of the hill and down into the village.

CHAPTER SEVENTEEN

THROWN clear by the force of the explosion, Jesse Fletcher floated face down in a pool of water three feet deep. Most of his clothing had been burned away and several ribs showed through the charred flesh of his back.

Gregory and Vanbrugh waded forward and turned him over. The strange thing was that his face was unmarked except for the bruises left by his clash with Rogan and his eyes stared vacantly into eternity, fixed for all time.

'Do you know him?' Gregory asked.

Vanbrugh shook his head. 'He's a new one on me.'

The truck was still burning furiously and as they approached, they became aware at once of the sickly sweet stench of burning flesh.

A constable turned, his face wrinkling in disgust. 'One of them's still in the cab, sir. You can just see him if you bend down.'

In the intense heat, things seemed to shimmer, to lose definition and the figure which lay doubled up, one arm reaching out through the crumpled window, no longer seemed human.

'A nasty way to go,' Gregory said.

Vanbrugh nodded and they stumbled across the stream, knee-deep in ice-cold water to where another constable knelt beside a body in the wet grass.

As they approached, he stood up and turned. 'Nothing doing here, sir. His neck's broke. Must have been thrown out of the back when the truck first landed.'

Jack Pope lay on his back, one arm bent, fingers curling slightly. His eyes had retracted slightly and his head lolled unnaturally to one side.

'What about this one?' Gregory said.

'Jack Pope. He's the one who shared a cell with Rogan.'

'The ex-policeman?'

'That's him.'

They turned and Vanbrugh shielded his eyes from the rain with one hand and watched half a dozen men move up the mountainside above the road in a thin line. Gregory gave a sudden grunt and pointed.

'There he is, just below the ridge.'

Vanbrugh caught a brief glimpse of Morgan moving fast, several hundred feet above his pursuers. A moment later he went over the ridge and disappeared.

'Red hair,' Gregory said. 'At least we know that much about the bastard.'

So it wasn't Sean Rogan—Vanbrugh moved back across the stream and picked up a piece of red mailbag canvas that shredded in his hands, still smouldering.

'Just about settles it,' Gregory said.

'Looks like it.'

They climbed the steep slope and arrived back on the road in time to see the wounded constable being lifted into the rear of the Land-Rover. His face was twisted with pain, but he managed a grin when Gregory lit a cigarette for him and stuck it in his mouth.

'How is it?'

The constable gingerly touched the blood-soaked bandage that encircled his right thigh above the knee. 'Bloody awful, but I'll survive, sir.'

'Good man,' Gregory said. 'Don't worry. We'll lay him by the heels.'

As the Land-Rover moved away, a police car came

down the road from the direction of the farm and braked to a halt. Sergeant Dwyer jumped out.

'Any luck?' Vanbrugh said.

'Not a soul to be seen, sir, but they've certainly been having themselves a high old time. Someone's been shooting the place up.'

'Now what in the hell is that supposed to mean?' Vanbrugh said, frowning.

'A hundred and forty thousand is a hell of a lot of money,' Gregory said. 'Maybe somebody wanted a bigger slice of the cake.' He turned to Dwyer. 'What about the car we heard driving away?'

'We found it a mile or so further on where the road peters out in the ruins of an old mining village. A green Morris Oxford shooting brake.'

'No sign of the occupants?'

'Not a smell. There's a sergeant and two men up there now, but they're going to need help.'

Vanbrugh turned to Gregory. 'Didn't you say there was no other way out of the valley?'

Gregory nodded. 'Not by road, but any reasonably active person could cross the mountain on foot.' He took a map from his pocket and opened it. 'You can see the village here and the old workings on the other side.'

Vanbrugh studied the map for a moment and pointed to the two dotted lines that marked the course of the Long Cut under the mountain. 'What's this? A canal?'

'It certainly looks like it. Probably used to ship ore through to the next valley in the old days.'

'If it were still navigable, it would make a convenient back door. The sooner it's plugged the better.'

Gregory moved to the nearest car and contacted headquarters on the radio. Vanbrugh looked up at the mountainside. The half dozen policemen were just below the ridge and they went over one by one as he watched.

And a fat lot of good it'll do them, he told himself. *He'll be half a mile down the other side of the mountain by now and still running.*

Dwyer moved to join him. 'Anyone we know down there, sir?'

'Jack Pope,' Vanbrugh said. 'I couldn't identify the other two. One of them was burned to a crisp anyway.'

'It couldn't have been Rogan, then?'

'I don't think so. Too small.'

Gregory came back from the patrol car. 'They're giving us every spare car and man they've got to cover the immediate area.'

'What about the other valley?'

'There are two cars on the way there now.' Gregory wiped rain from his face and smiled confidently. 'We're bound to get them, you know. This isn't the big city with a maze of back streets to hide in. There are damned few roads round here. We can seal them all with no trouble at all.'

'Then we've nothing to worry about,' Vanbrugh said. 'I'd like to take a quick look over the farm now if that's all right with you.'

'What about this fellow Soames? Should I have him brought up here? Perhaps we could squeeze something useful out of him.'

'A damned good idea,' Vanbrugh said. 'At least we might get a few answers to some rather puzzling questions,' and he turned and followed Dwyer through the heavy rain towards the patrol car.

Soames' agile brain was working overtime, seeking a way out of the predicament in which he found himself as the patrol car turned off the Ambleside road and moved up the track towards Scardale.

His wrists were handcuffed together and a constable sat on either side of him. As they came to the place where the accident had occurred, the driver slowed to ease past the parked vehicles and several men staggered over the edge of the road carrying a stretcher.

Soames stared out at the shapeless form beneath the blanket. An arm hung down to the ground, flesh peeling from the fingers and he shuddered as the wind carried the sickly sweet smell through the open window.

The young constable on his right turned and looked at him coldly. 'You'll be lucky to get away with fifteen years for this little lot.'

Soames felt suddenly sick. Only once in his career had he been stupid enough to step just too far over the shadow line between what was legal and what wasn't. The subsequent experience had not been pleasant.

It came to him, with a thrill of horror, that this time he had gone in over his head and his mouth went dry. The car turned in through the gate and braked beside another which stood outside the farmhouse door.

The two policemen pulled him out and he followed them inside and along the narrow whitewashed passage. It was like something out of a bad dream and the look on the faces of the three men who waited for him in the sitting room didn't make him feel any better.

Vanbrugh examined him briefly. 'Henry Soames?'

Soames moistened dry lips. 'That's right. I'd like to know why I've been brought here.' He added feebly, 'I have my rights. I demand to see a solicitor.'

'A short while ago, a young policeman was shot by one of your pals,' Vanbrugh cut in coldly. 'A man with red hair. If that boy dies, I'll see you in the dock as an accessory to murder.'

Soames struggled for breath as fear turned his bowels to water. Finally he managed to speak. 'Morgan, that's the man you want. Harry Morgan. He's the one with red hair.'

'Who else was in on this?'

Soames stumbled over his words in his eagerness to get them out. 'Jesse Fletcher. He and Morgan came up together from Manchester. And there was the man who owns this farm, Costello.'

'And his niece?'

'That's right.'

'What about Jack Pope?' Dwyer put in.

Soames turned to him eagerly. 'Oh, yes, he was in on it, too.'

'When you visited Sean Rogan in prison, it was to arrange details of his escape?' Vanbrugh demanded.

'That's right. On the night he got out, Pope was waiting with a car and a change of clothes.'

'Who laid everything on?'

'A man called Colum O'More.'

Gregory frowned and looked at Vanbrugh. 'That's a familiar name.'

'It should be,' Vanbrugh said. 'He was a big man in the I.R.A. in the thirties and during the early part of the war.' He turned back to Soames. 'So the I.R.A. are in this after all? Funds for the Organization, I suppose?'

'That's what Rogan believed.'

'Let me get this straight,' Vanbrugh said. 'Morgan and Fletcher were working for wages, right?'

'Five thousand apiece. Rogan was just working off a debt. O'More persuaded him that he owed the Organization one last favour for breaking him out.'

'So the rest of the haul goes to I.R.A. funds?'

'That's what O'More told Rogan.'

'But you know different?'

'You're telling me. The old spider wants the bloody lot for himself.'

Vanbrugh shook his head. 'It won't wash, Soames. I know Colum O'More, everything about him. He isn't the type to pull a stroke like that.'

Soames shrugged. 'He's a sick man, cancer or something. That kind of thing changes people.'

Gregory looked at Vanbrugh quickly. 'I'll buy that.'

Vanbrugh nodded. 'Where's O'More now?'

Soames moistened his lips. 'Can we make a deal?'

'I wouldn't cut you down if you were hanging,' Vanbrugh said calmly. 'Now tell me where O'More is or I'll kick you from here to the door and back again.'

'He's at an old farm just off the coast road near Whitbeck,' Soames said sullenly. 'Marsh-End, it's called.'

'Anyone with him?'

Soames shook his head. 'He's on his own. Rogan was supposed to drive over tomorrow with the money.'

'But you and your friends had ideas of your own about that?' Vanbrugh turned to Gregory. 'At least that gives us some sort of explanation for the shooting that's been going on here. They probably tried to get their hands on the loot and Rogan objected. Do you know this place, Marsh-End?'

'No, but I know Whitbeck. It'll take us about forty-five minutes to get there in weather like this.'

'Then let's get moving.'

Vanbrugh walked out quickly and Gregory and Dwyer went after him. Soames looked around him hurriedly for a possible exit and a middle-aged police sergeant came through the door, a broad grin on his face.

'Didn't think we'd forget you, did you?'

In that moment the full realization of what had happened to him hit Soames with sickening force. Outside the patrol car moved away carrying Vanbrugh, Gregory and Dwyer. As he stood there listening to the sound of the engine fade into the distance, he felt more lonely than he had ever felt in his life before.

The ditch was half-full of water and Morgan waded along it for some fifty yards, then darted across to the shelter of the fir trees on the other side. A few moments later, a police car swept by, followed by another.

By now, they would have sealed every main road through the mountains, that much was obvious. It would take a miracle to get through and yet he had to reach the coast. His one chance of escape lay at Marsh-End with Colum O'More.

As he started to work his way through the plantation of firs, a motorcyclist passed along the main road and slowed to a halt thirty or forty yards further on. Morgan went forward cautiously and paused behind a bush.

A police motorcyclist stood beside an A.A. box, his

142

machine parked a few feet away. He was examining a map. As Morgan watched, he slipped a cigarette into his mouth and flicked a lighter.

Morgan didn't even think about it. He gripped his revolver by the barrel, jumped forward and struck hard at the nape of the neck. The policeman gave a stifled cry and slumped to his knees. Morgan grabbed him by the shoulders and pulled him back into the bushes. Then he ran out into the road, kicked the stand from under the motorcycle and pushed it under cover in the plantation.

It took him five minutes to strip the policeman and dress in his uniform. When he was ready, he fastened the man's wrists behind him with his belt and moved towards the motorcycle.

At that moment, another patrol car swept by. He waited until the sound of its engine had faded into the distance, then ran the machine out into the road, mounted it and kicked the starter. As the engine roared into life, he pulled down the goggles and rode away.

Half a mile further on he came to a bridge. On the other side a police car was parked half across the road leaving room for single line traffic only and two constables blocked the way. Morgan changed down and started to slow, at the same time getting ready to accelerate.

There was no need. As he went over the bridge, the two constables moved out of the way and one of them waved a hand casually. It was as easy as that. Morgan changed into top gear and sped away into the rain.

CHAPTER EIGHTEEN

WHEN Rogan cut the engine and jumped out of the shooting brake, there was no sign of Brendan and the rain hissing down into the water of the dam was the only sound.

Hannah moved around the brake to join him. 'I wonder where he is?'

'God knows, but we've got to get moving. If we don't get through the tunnel and down to Ambleside Road within fifteen minutes, we've had it.'

There was a sudden restless baaing and several sheep ran between the ruined houses, scattering to avoid Brendan who raced after them brandishing a stick. They plunged up the mountainside and he paused, slightly out of breath, and grinned.

'I thought I'd better set them free.'

'Never mind about them now, we've got to get going. Where are the mailbags?'

'I put them in the punt, Mr. Rogan.'

They hurried round the side of the dam and through the clump of trees that masked the old landing stage. Brendan had moored the punt to a rusty iron ring and several inches of water slopped in the bottom. The mailbags were in the prow where it was dry, and Hannah sat down on them. Rogan crouched in the centre and Brendan shoved off from the rear.

The sound of the rain faded as they moved into the cold darkness and he looked at his watch. It was almost five o'clock and it wasn't dark till seven thirty, which didn't help. It wouldn't take the police long to work out what had happened when they found the shooting brake. One fast patrol car to block the end of the other valley was all that it would take. Certainly, if Dick Vanbrugh was in on things, the hunt was up with a vengeance.

And what happened if the jeep wasn't there? But he pushed that thought away from him. If they could get down to the Ambleside road and reach the track that led between Rydal Water and Grasmere to Elterwater they might stand a chance. Beyond was the lonely road over Wrynose and old packhorse tracks that crossed over the fells to the coast, places where only a jeep or a similar vehicle could go.

They drifted out into the heavy rain and bumped against the side of the stone landing stage. Brendan scrambled up and fastened the line, then gave Hannah a hand and Rogan passed up the two mailbags.

Brendan ran on ahead through the trees and Rogan and the girl followed. When they reached the old stable, the boy had already got the doors open, revealing the jeep.

He opened the rear door and Rogan heaved the two mailbags inside. 'All right, let's get moving.'

Brendan scrambled into the rear, Hannah got into the passenger seat and Rogan slid behind the wheel. He pulled out the choke and pressed the starter and the engine turned over at once. In one smooth movement he reversed out of the stable, swung the wheel, moved into first gear and roared down the track towards the mouth of the valley.

'We'll try that route you told me about on Wednesday,' he said to Hannah.

'Do we stand a chance?'

'All depends on how quickly they get a car round to this side. If we can reach that track you told me about leading across to Elterwater and get off the main road, we might surprise them yet.'

He drove very fast, his foot hard against the boards and the jeep responded magnificently. Five minutes later, they turned up through a clump of fir trees and reached the main road.

Rogan barely paused, swung the wheel to the right and

drove along the road towards Rydal. 'How far?' he shouted above the roaring of the engine.

'Half a mile, no more.'

Rain hammered against the windscreen so hard that the wipers had difficulty in coping. He leaned forward anxiously as a truck passed them going the opposite way and then Hannah was tugging at his arm.

He saw the gate in a clump of fir trees in the same moment and braked, skidding a little. As he swung the wheel and stopped, the girl jumped down and opened the gate. Rogan drove through and waited for her to close it again. A moment later, they were moving on through the trees and when he looked in the mirror, he could no longer see the road.

His throat was dry and there was sweat on his forehead. His hand trembled slightly when he raised it to brush away the sweat.

'Would you look at that, now? I've got the shakes.' He gave her a quick grin. 'Maybe I'm getting too old for this sort of caper.'

'That'll be the day.'

She produced matches and cigarettes from one of her pockets, lit one and put it in his mouth. Rogan inhaled deeply and sighed. 'I needed that.'

'First hurdle over safely,' she said.

He nodded. 'That's about the size of it. How do you feel?'

'As if I'm really crashing out of something for the first time in my life.'

'Keep on believing that and it'll come true.'

They crossed the bridge and he changed down and drove along the narrow track between the trees. It took them no more than three or four minutes to reach the Elterwater road, another five to reach the village itself. The streets were deserted in the heavy rain and he drove quietly through, following Hannah's directions until, at Eltermere, he turned into a side road that skirted Little Langdale village. A quarter of an hour after leaving the

Ambleside road, they were moving alongside Little Langdale Tarn and starting the long climb up to Wrynose.

The road lifted steeply before them, mist crowding in across the mountains, and the jeep climbed steadily, its engine deepening to a full-throated roar as he changed down through the gears.

Gradually, the mist enfolded them, and when they reached the top of the pass visibility was down to twenty or thirty yards. Rogan stayed in a low gear on the way down the steep hill to Wrynose Bottom and they followed the course of the Duddon River. Ten minutes later, they came to the place where the road forked, one arm climbing to Hard Knott, the other following the valley to Seathwaite and Ulpha.

'Give me another cigarette,' he said.

The girl lit one and put it in his mouth and Brendan leaned over the back of the bench seat. 'H-how are we doing, Mr. Rogan?'

'So far, so good, son.' Rogan pulled in at the side of the road. 'Let's have another look at that map.'

He examined it quickly, a slight frown on his face. 'No way round Seathwaite and Ulpha from the looks of things.'

'Are you expecting trouble?' Hannah said.

'It's possible. They've had plenty of time to pass the word around by now.'

She had another look at the map and traced a line across the fells. 'There's an unfenced road here. It won't be very good but it runs across Thwaites Fell to the coast. We'd still have to go through Ulpha, but it would cut out the other places.'

'Where does it start?'

'Beckfoot, a couple of miles on the far side of Ulpha.'

'Good enough.'

He drove away quickly, and as they passed through the little village of Seathwaite the mist seemed to be thinning a little, but the rain continued to fall relentlessly as they dropped down through the pleasant wooded valley.

The main street was deserted, but as they approached the village inn, Hannah clutched Rogan's arm tightly. A police sergeant in peaked cap and heavy blue raincoat stood on the steps talking to a middle-aged woman.

Rogan drove steadily past, but when he glanced in the mirror, they were both watching the jeep as it moved away along the main street. The sergeant turned and said something to the woman and they went into the inn quickly.

'Did you see that?' Hannah said.

Rogan nodded grimly. 'We'll have to take that un-fenced road over the top now. No choice.'

He pushed his foot down hard until the needle flickered on sixty and the old jeep roared along the road, spurning the gravel. It took them no more than two or three minutes to reach Beckfoot and he braked, and flung the jeep into the side turning.

They climbed into another world, grey and sombre, dark crags, dripping with moisture, looming out of the mist on either hand. The road stretched before them, unfenced, but surprisingly well surfaced and the jeep slowed as the slope lifted before them.

The roaring of the engine in low gear was almost un-bearable and the old aluminium body rattled alarm-ingly. Rogan checked the petrol gauge and saw they were down to the last gallon.

'How far have we got to go?' he shouted.

Hannah had another look at the map. 'About six miles to Bootle, but we don't need to go right in. There's a track branching down to the coast road. A mile, maybe two, to Marsh-End. Have we enough petrol?'

He nodded and changed into top gear as they breasted the slope and moved past Mere Crags across a jagged plateau, shrouded in fog.

It came to him, with something like surprise, that they had nearly made it, that with any kind of luck at all another ten minutes, fifteen at the most, should see them at Marsh-End. The road started to drop steeply into a grey void and he took it on the run, braking on the corners instead of changing to a low gear.

About a quarter of a mile outside Bootle they came to a finger-post sign carrying the legend *Whicham,* and turned into a narrow, rutted track that brought them on to the coast road three or four minutes later.

Mist drifted in across the marsh carrying the good salt smell of the sea, and Rogan's spirits lifted. The signpost for Marsh-End loomed out of the gloom. He turned into the track and they lurched over the rutted surface through the trees beside the creek and rolled to a halt in the yard.

When he switched off the engine and turned to Hannah her eyes were shining. 'So we made it after all?'

He grinned and squeezed her hands. 'I hope you're a good sailor. It's a rough crossing in a small boat.'

Fog rolled in across the marsh, pushed by the wind, and he opened the door and got out. Brendan pulled the mailbags to the ground and dragged them round to him. The house was strangely quiet and the windows stared blindly down at them like dark eyes. Rogan frowned, picked up the mailbags and crossed to the door. Hannah opened it for him and led the way along the narrow passage.

Colum O'More was in the easy chair by the fire, his head lolling to one side. As Rogan dropped the mailbags, Hannah moved forward and examined the old man quickly.

'Is he dead?' Rogan said.

She shook her head. 'He's very cold, though.'

There was no fire in the grate and Rogan went to the sideboard, opened it and found a bottle of Irish whiskey. He half filled a glass, went back to the chair and forced a little of it between the old man's lips.

Colum O'More coughed, his head shaking from side to side and then his eyes opened suddenly. He looked at Rogan blankly for a moment and recognition dawned.

'Sean boy,' he said in Irish. 'Is it yourself?'

'And none other, Colum Oge,' Rogan answered in the same language.

The old man's eyes moved to Hannah and he smiled. 'You too, girl, dear.'

She looked desperately at Rogan. 'I don't understand?'

'Give him a moment to pull himself together.'

O'More ran a hand over his face, shook himself and reached for the glass of whiskey. He took it down with a single swallow and shuddered. 'God save us all, but that's better,' he said in English.

When he looked up there was a different expression in his eyes and he seemed more alert. 'But what are you doing here? What's gone wrong?'

'We're a day early, that's all,' Rogan said, 'and every peeler in the country on the prowl for us. We'll have to be moving, Colum.'

'You've pulled it off?'

Rogan dumped the two mailbags on the table. 'That we have.'

The old man stared at him incredulously. 'What time is it?'

'A little after seven.'

'But that can't be.' Colum O'More shook his head vigorously. 'I had a bad attack just after I got up this morning so I took some of my pills. Maybe more than I should have done.'

'Now that, I can believe. Are your things packed?'

'There's a suitcase in the bedroom, it's got everything I need.'

Rogan turned to Hannah. 'Make him a hot drink. I'll send Brendan on ahead to the boat with the suitcase. There are one or two things he can be doing to help us make a quick exit.'

Hannah nodded and went out and Rogan got the suitcase from the bedroom and took Brendan across the courtyard at the rear of the farm to where the track through the marsh began.

150

'You'll come to a stone causeway a couple of hundred yards from here,' he said. 'Just beyond it, there's a narrower path to the right. Follow that and you'll come to a motor launch. She's tied fore and aft. Cast off and hold her ready on a single line. We'll be along in ten minutes.'

The boy nodded eagerly and moved away, the case bumping against his right leg. Rogan went back into the house. O'More still sat in his chair by the fire and as Rogan entered the room, Hannah came in from the kitchen with a coffee pot and cups on a tray.

'What happens when we get to Ireland?' she said as she started to pour. 'Do we just sail boldly in?'

Colum O'More chuckled. 'Hardly that, girl. There's a quiet place I know and good friends not far away. That's where I'll be leaving you and Sean.'

She looked up at Rogan. 'Then what?'

'We'll go to my father's place in Kerry. I never made things easy for a peeler in my life, not even an Irish one. They can come for me, there.'

Her face clouded over at once. 'Prison again?'

O'More laughed harshly. 'But not for long, girl, make no mistake about that. What you might call a necessary formality. You'll be back in his arms inside a month.'

She looked up at Rogan anxiously. 'Is that the truth?'

'Since when have I lied to you?' Rogan kissed her gently on the forehead. 'Get your coat on, we'd better be making a move.'

He felt her stiffen in his arms as she looked behind him and a cold wind gently touched him on the back of the neck. In the mirror above the mantelpiece, he saw the door swing open, framing a police motorcyclist, strangely anonymous, broad goggles masking his eyes beneath the peak of the white uniform crash helmet.

He unfastened his chin strap, pulled off his helmet and goggles and Harry Morgan smiled out at them.

CHAPTER NINETEEN

MORGAN's face was lined with fatigue and the revolver he was holding trembled slightly. 'Make any kind of a wrong move and I'll kill you, I swear it,' he said harshly. 'Clasp your hands behind your neck.'

He moved to the table and patted the mailbags with his free hand. 'So the two we grabbed back there at the farm were dummies? I've got to hand it to you for nerve, Rogan. Turn round.'

Rogan did as he was told. When he raised his arms, his jacket gaped, revealing the Colt automatic in his waistband.

Morgan nodded to Hannah. 'Take out his shooter with your left hand and toss it across.' She hesitated and he raised the revolver quickly. 'I shot a copper back there at Scardale. I've nothing to lose now.'

'Do as he says,' Rogan told her.

She reached for the automatic with her left hand and threw it across awkwardly. Morgan grabbed for it, missed, and the gun skidded across the floor and came to rest under the table.

She took an involuntary step forward and he shook his head. 'Leave it.'

Rogan lowered his hands. 'What happens now?'

'I'm going to take a little boat trip, just me and the old man here like he arranged with Soames.'

Hannah sucked in her breath sharply.

Rogan turned and looked down at Colum O'More, a frown on his face. 'What's he talking about?'

The skin of the old man's face tightened across the cheekbones and his eyes were dark holes as he glared at Morgan. 'He's trying to make trouble, can't you see that?'

'You must be losing your touch, Rogan,' Morgan

jeered. 'The old bastard's been stringing you along from the beginning. He didn't want funds for his blasted Organization. He wanted a stake for his old age. He used you, Rogan, and Soames found out about it.'

'Is it true?' Rogan said calmly.

O'More looked down at the floor and Morgan laughed again. 'Is it true, the man says. That's why we were supposed to cut you out back at the farm. We were all going to meet here tomorrow and divvy up if things hadn't gone sour.'

O'More looked up sharply. 'I knew nothing of that, Sean, nothing about any plans concerning you. Soames found out, it's true, and threatened to tell you unless I cut him in. But that's as far as it went.'

'Funds for the Organization, you said.'

'I'd have seen you all right, lad.'

'A high price to pay for my good name.' Rogan tapped his chest. 'I am Sean Rogan, a soldier of the Irish Republican Army and no thief.'

'To hell with the Irish Republican Army.' The old man slammed his stick hard against the floor. 'Forty years, Sean Rogan. Forty years I've given to the Organization. Twenty of those I've served in gaol on both sides of the water and what have I got to show for it?' He coughed harshly, struggling for breath, and pulled at his collar. 'Old and broken, my lungs rotting. By God, I'll pass the time left to me in comfort or know the reason why.'

Rogan shook his head and there was something close to compassion on his face. 'It won't work, Colum. That kind of thing never does.'

'Don't let him kid you, old man,' Morgan said.

He took a clasp knife from his pocket, opened the blade with his teeth and slashed through the cord binding the neck of one of the bags. He dropped the knife on the table, put a hand inside and pulled out a packet of notes.

He threw it at Rogan who grabbed it instinctively.

153

'How much is that, Rogan? Five hundred, a thousand? He patted the bag. 'Lots more in here, big man, and you're going to carry them down to the boat for me.'

Rogan examined the bundle of notes in his hand and a slow smile spread across his face. 'If the rest are like these there wouldn't be much point.' He dropped the bundle into O'More's lap. 'What do you think, Colum?'

Colum O'More pulled out several pound notes and held them up to the light. His eyes widened. 'Holy Mother of God, they're perforated, every last one of them.'

He passed one to Hannah who held it to the light, then looked at Rogan, surprise on her face. 'What does it mean?'

'They were talking about it in the prison a month or two back,' he said. 'A trick some of the banks are using now if they're shipping old notes in quantity for repulping. They run them through an electronic machine that perforates each one with a code number in large letters as you can see.'

'Making them useless?'

'As legal tender. That's the general idea.'

'What the hell are you talking about?'

Morgan upended the mailbag on the table, scattering packets to the floor. He examined one feverishly and then another and another. When he turned, his face was very white.

'They're all the same, every damned one.'

'This just isn't your day, Morgan,' Rogan said.

Colum O'More let out a great gust of laughter. 'If you could see your face, you scut. Somehow, it makes the whole damned thing worth while.'

'This is your fault, you bastard,' Morgan spat at him. 'The whole bloody thing was a waste of time from the start. We'd have known that if your information had been right.'

'We all make mistakes, lad,' Colum O'More said, and pushed himself up.

Morgan shot him twice in the body, the force of the bullets knocking him back into the chair. As Hannah screamed, Rogan flung himself headlong under the table, his hand reaching for the butt of the automatic.

Morgan jumped back to get a clear view of him, but he was too late. Rogan's first shot caught him in the chest, the second in the stomach, knocking him back against the wall. He dropped his revolver and crumpled to his knees, his face wiped clean of all expression, then fell forward.

Colum O'More was doubled over in pain. Hannah, on her knees beside him, tried to lift his head. Rogan dropped the automatic on the table and pushed the old man back into his chair. His eyes were tightly closed, teeth clenched against the pain and his forehead was beaded with sweat.

Rogan shook him gently. 'Colum, listen to me. How bad is it?'

The old man opened his eyes and Death stared out at them. 'As bad as it's ever likely to get, lad.' He looked beyond them into space. 'The long road I've walked, a road I was proud to be on, and now this.' He coughed and a trickle of blood oozed from the corner of his mouth. 'It wasn't me, Sean, it wasn't the Big Man. It was the sickness inside me. I think a little of it must have touched my brain as well.'

Rogan stood up and turned to Hannah. 'Hang on here. I'm going for a doctor.'

'You're wasting your time,' Colum O'More called and Rogan stepped over Harry Morgan, and moved along the passage.

He heard the cars up on the main road as he opened the outside door and the furious jangle of the bell through the trees, muffled by the fog, as the first one braked hard and swung into the track. He slammed the door shut, bolted it and ran back into the living room.

'The peelers are here.' He grabbed Hannah by the arm, ran her into the kitchen and wrenched open the back door. 'You know the way to the boat. Get down

155

there fast and wait for me.'

She tried to protest and he shook her brutally. 'Do as you're told. Haven't I enough to worry about?'

He pushed her into the fog, slammed the door and ran back into the living room. 'They'll be here soon, Colum. They'll be able to do more for you than I can.'

'There's no help for me on top of earth,' the old man said through clenched teeth, 'but there is for you. Now pass me that gun and get to hell out of here. Harry Morgan's death can be on my conscience, not yours.'

'For God's sake, Colum . . .'

'That's an order, damn you,' the old man spat at him. As Rogan passed him the gun a car braked outside and footsteps pounded across the cobbles. 'Get out of it!' Colum O'More shouted and Rogan ran through the kitchen and wrenched open the back door.

He was halfway across the yard when a young constable came round the corner on a dead run. Rogan swerved, his fist glanced off a cheekbone and the man grunted and went down. As cries broke out behind, he reached the shelter of the trees and was swallowed up by the fog.

Morgan pushed himself up slowly and fell back against the wall. His entire body seemed to be one great pain and there was blood in his mouth. He focused on Colum O'More and gave him a ghastly grin.

'I'll hang on, you old bastard. Long enough to make sure Rogan swings for me.'

'Is that a fact now?' Colum O'More said and shot him through the head. As the outside door gave, the automatic slipped from his grasp and he fell forward.

Vanbrugh was first through the door, Gregory close behind. He dropped to one knee beside the old man, raising his head gently, but Colum O'More stared blindly into eternity.

'This one's had it,' Gregory said, getting to his feet beside Morgan. 'What about him?'

Vanbrugh shook his head and picked up one of the packets of banknotes. 'Didn't do anybody much good, this little lot, did it?'

Dwyer came in from the kitchen in a hurry. 'Someone made a run for it through the back door and clouted a constable. Sounds like Rogan.'

'Better get after him then,' Gregory said.

Vanbrugh led the way through the kitchen and across the yard. It was almost nightfall, and the fog drifting through the trees turned the marsh into a place of shadows.

'You round up every man you can,' he told Gregory. 'Dwyer and I'll go straight in after him. He can't have gone very far.'

Gregory turned, blowing his whistle sharply and Vanbrugh ran forward into the trees, Dwyer at his heels. Branches lashed against his face and he held up an arm to ward them off and stumbled on. Within a few moments they came to a narrow track that led across a stone causeway. On the other side, there was a turning to the left through tangled undergrowth and Vanbrugh paused, struggling for breath.

'I'll try this one, you go on ahead. Whatever happens, don't try to take him on your own. You aren't that good. If you catch sight of him, blow your whistle and I'll come running.'

Dwyer nodded and moved into the fog and Vanbrugh turned into the track through the undergrowth and started to run.

Rogan could hear the police whistle muffled by the fog, but distinctive enough for all that, and he put down his head and ran, crashing through a plantation of young firs, the branches whipping his sides. He tripped and fell, rolling down a small incline and again heard the police whistle.

He got to his feet, staggered forward and blundered through a fringe of bushes into the side turning that led down to the creek. He started to run, his chest heaving

157

painfully, and burst through the trees on to the bank of the creek beside the launch a few moments later.

Hannah ran to meet him, her face a pale blur in the evening light. 'Are you all right?'

'Never mind me,' he said. 'There are peelers all over the place. Get on board.'

Brendan stood in the stern with a ten foot pole, hopping with excitement. 'Are we ready to go, Mr. Rogan? Shall I give the engine a turn?'

'And attract everyone for miles around?' Rogan shook his head. 'We'll let the tide take us out through the estuary.'

He ran to the single line that still held the launch to land and cast off. The vessel swung out from the bank at once, caught by the tide, and Hannah called anxiously, 'Quickly, Sean.'

As Rogan took a step forward, Vanbrugh ran out of the undergrowth and cannoned into him. They rolled over and over on the ground, fetching up against a line of old rotting palings, Rogan on top. His great hands fastened around the policeman's throat and then he recognized him. He released his grip and got to his feet.

'Get up.'

They stood facing each other in the half-light, police whistles sounding monotonously from every part of the marsh, and Hannah gave a stifled cry.

Vanbrugh looked at her, shadowy and insubstantial in the fog as the launch drifted away, then he turned back to Rogan.

'Well, get moving, for Christ's sake!'

Rogan plunged into the water. He waded out to the launch, pulled himself up over the rail and took the pole from the boy. He turned and looked back at Vanbrugh for a long moment, then raised his hand in a half salute and poled the launch into the fog.

Vanbrugh stood there staring into the grey void and, after a while, Dwyer arrived. 'Any sign of him, sir?'

Vanbrugh shook his head. 'Got a cigarette?'

Dwyer took out his case. As he was giving him a light, there was the faint, distant rumble of an engine breaking into life.

He frowned. 'Did you hear that, sir?'

Vanbrugh stood listening, head on one side. He shook his head. 'I didn't hear a damned thing, Sergeant. Come on, we're wasting our time here.'

He turned and led the way back along the path through the undergrowth.

As the launch drifted out of the estuary, waves started to slap against her hull and Rogan pressed the starter. The powerful diesel engines rumbled into life and he took the launch in a long sweeping curve out past the last point of land into the open sea.

He turned and smiled down at Hannah standing there in the cockpit beside him, and slipped an arm around her waist, pulling her close. For the first time in his life he felt as if he were really crashing out of something.

ALSO BY JACK HIGGINS
IN CORONET

All these books are available at your local bookshop or newsagent, or can be ordered direct from the publisher. Just tick the titles you want and fill in the form below.

Prices and availability subject to change without notice.

CORONET BOOKS, P.O. Box 11, Falmouth, Cornwall.

Please send cheque or postal order, and allow the following for postage and packing:

U.K.—45p for one book, plus 20p for the second book, and 14p for each additional book ordered up to a £1.63 maximum.

B.F.P.O. and EIRE—45p for the first book, plus 20p for the second book, and 14p per copy for the next 7 books, 8p per book thereafter.

OTHER OVERSEAS CUSTOMERS—75p for the first book, plus 21p per copy for each additional book.

Name ....

Address ....

....